Valuing Gold

Endorsements

Sometimes we must be dragged—forcefully—into our destiny. Cynthia L. Simmons artfully depicts the "every woman" story of how to find our divine purpose rather than looking away at the trouble around us. Her love of history is evident in how she paints *Valuing Gold*'s picture of conflict and contrasts. Southern grace and brutal war. Politics and principles. Murder and freedom. All packaged together in a surprising mystery. A worthy read.

—**Terri Gillespie**, award-winning author of *She Does Good Hair*

Having worked at a bank for two summers during college, I was intrigued with the historical lessons of the banking business I learned while reading Cynthia L. Simmons's *Valuing Gold*, set in 1862 in Chattanooga, Tennessee. Cynthia manages to weave the scriptural lesson of valuing God's truth between the pages of the story without preaching or pointing fingers.

—**Julie Lavender**, author of *365 Ways to Love Your Children: Turning Little Moments into Lasting Memories (Revell)*

Valuing Gold, a compelling Civil War novel, includes romance, murder, and mystery while demonstrating the value of gold during this turbulent period of history.

—**Susan U. Neal**, RN, MBA, MHS, Bbest-selling author of *7 Steps to Get Off Sugar and Carbohydrates*

I felt as if I were reading *Gone with the Wind*. In *Valuing Gold*, Simmons's delightful descriptions, welcoming characters, and intriguing plot took me to the world of the Civil War. I lived the danger, pathos, yet heartfelt journeys of those caught in the winds of change and uncertainty. Through Simmons's talented creative fiction pen, the world of a long-gone era is remembered. I love everything Simmons writes, and I'm so glad I could enjoy this riveting tale.

—**Kathy Collard Miller**, author of over fifty-five books including *God's Intriguing Questions: 60 New Testament Devotions Revealing Jesus's Nature*. She is also an international speaker who has spoken in nine foreign countries and over thirty USA states.

Cynthia L. Simmons's passion for Civil War history comes through in this novel about people whose lives are thrown into turmoil at the outset of the conflict. This is a fast-paced story with an intriguing element of mystery.

—**Dr. Rebecca Price Janney**, award-winning author of twenty-four books, historian, speaker

Multi-talented author Cynthia L. Simmons brings to life the people who lived, loved, and championed the polarized sides of the American Civil War. The prequel to her first novel in the series, *Valuing Gold* illuminates the life-changing decisions made when our nation was at a crossroads. As the refining fire of political conflict increased, would leaders in the financial community come through as gold?

—**PeggySue Wells**, bestselling author of twenty-nine books including *Homeless for the Holidays* and *Chasing Sunrise*

Valuing Gold

Cynthia L. Simmons

PUBLISHING THE POSITIVE

ELK LAKE PUBLISHING INC
Plymouth, Massachusetts

Cover and Interior Design: Derinda Babcock

Editor(s): Marcie Bridges, Deb Haggerty

Author Represented By: WordWise Media Services

PUBLISHED BY: Elk Lake Publishing, Inc., 35 Dogwood Drive, Plymouth, MA 02360, 2020

Library Cataloging Data

Names: Simmons, Cynthia L. (Cynthia L. Simmons)

Valuing Gold / Cynthia L. Simmons

p. 23cm × 15cm (9in × 6 in.)

Identifiers: ISBN-13: 978-1-64949-080-3 (paperback) | 978-1-64949-081-0 (trade paperback) | 978-1-64949-08207 (e-book)

Key Words: Civil War, romance, mystery, banking, intrigue, murder, family relationships

LCCN: 2020948681 Fiction

To Charity and Emily,
who enjoy writing as much as I do.

Acknowledgments

Thanks goes to Mavian Arocha-Rowee for all her help and support.

Another big thanks goes to Linda Evans Shepherd for her encouragement.

Thanks to Derinda, Deb, Marcie, and the staff at Elk Lake Publishing for all their hard work

CHAPTER ONE

April 1861
The Roper Library

Mary Beth Roper held back a sigh as she turned another page of her book, even though she hadn't read the words. She loved everything about their library with its wall-sized bookcases, stocked with volumes. Normally, she would sink into the heavily padded chairs and escape, reading by the light of the oil lamps. But not tonight.

Fatigue lines on her father's face worried her. She kept glancing up at him where he sat at his mahogany desk across the room. He was working. He never rested. He seldom paused. "Papa, will you finish soon?"

Her father's green eyes glowed as he gazed at her. "I am making incredible progress." Her father never complained about the unending paperwork, but his hair had turned grayer. His vigor had waned, and they never took the air together now.

"Have you heard from Peter? I thought Mrs. Chandler had sent for him."

"I understand he is traveling home now." He tapped the stack of work beside him. "So, I must have the bank papers in order."

"I wish you didn't work so hard, Papa. Peter has his degree now and knows how to manage a bank."

"Of course." Her father adjusted his robe. "I shall be

delighted to see him. Such a fine young man."

"And new partner." Mary Beth had grown up around banking duties. "Is there anything I can do—"

A soft knock on the door interrupted them, and Maud, the Negro housekeeper, stepped inside. "I be sorry to be a botherin' you, but Miss Ida jus' arrived, and she bein' more upset than I ever seen her. Even at this late hour. I be havin' no idea what be eatin' at her, but she be a sayin' she must see you."

"I believe Ida needs you worse than I do." Her father chuckled. "Once you have calmed her, you should retire for the night, dearie."

She hurried over to kiss her father. "I shall check on you before bed."

If only he would rest.

Mary Beth opened the sitting room door and found Ida pacing around the sofa and overstuffed chairs. Her brow wrinkled, she mumbled to herself while fidgeting with her brown hair hanging loose from the bun on the back her head.

"Ida?" Mary Beth walked toward her friend wondering what it would take to allay her fears. "Shall I order some tea?"

Ida's brown eyes widened as she rushed toward Mary Beth, grabbing her arms. "Have you seen the fire? It's terrible."

"Fire?"

Ida pulled her into the hallway and opened the front door. "Look! You can see it on the mountain!

Stumbling outside and down her front steps, Mary Beth stared into the distance at a patch of orange above the trees. The fire must be huge if you could see it from here. "That's Lookout Mountain. What—?"

"Friends from Chattanooga called my father. You can see it better from downtown." Ida pulled her further into the street and toward the city where a throng had gathered. "The people on the mountain are secessionists who are rioting. If they enter the city, we could all be killed."

Mary Beth was thankful her father served as a banker rather than the town sheriff. She could hardly take her eyes from the blaze. "It's rather beautiful."

"My father said the war has started."

War. The word made Mary Beth's chest tighten, and she turned away from the sight to suck in air. She wanted the comfort of home and Papa. He could always assuage her anxiety. "Ida, I left without telling Father. At this hour, he will be alarmed. I must go back."

"Make sure you take precautions," Ida said, waving.

"We will." She hurried down the streets and burst into the front door, panting, as her father was coming down the hall toward the foyer, frowning.

"Maud said you left, and I worried about you being in town this late."

Mary Beth threw herself into his arms and relaxed, listening to his heartbeat and smelling his shaving soap. "There's a fire on Lookout Mountain. Ida says they are secessionists who believe the war has started."

"Hmm." He rubbed her back. "Chattanooga is pro-

Union, but I shall investigate."

"Tomorrow?" Her heart sped up. Her father should rest after all the work he'd done today. If he left, he might be in danger too.

He kissed the top of her head and laughed. "Dearie, you'd best go to bed. I shall see to the war—if there is one."

"But you'll tell me what you find out. Please?"

Her father hugged her once more and walked away without answering.

THE NEXT MORNING
NEW YORK

The smell of coffee, bacon, and the clatter of plates accosted Peter Chandler as he walked into the hotel restaurant. Half the tables stood empty, but he had risen early to have breakfast before meeting with clients.

Peter had already had enough traveling after crossing the ocean, but he still had a long trip to Chattanooga. A couple more days here, and he would be caught up on sleep before leaving for home.

"A table for one?" A waiter dressed in a white apron bowed slightly toward Peter.

Peter nodded. Once seated at a small cloth-covered table, the waiter offered him a menu and a newspaper. With his stomach growling, he rejected the menu, ordered a breakfast of flapjacks and coffee, then settled in his seat with the newspaper. The headlines, however, destroyed his appetite.

**SOUTH CAROLINA FIRES ON FORT SUMTER.
LINCOLN SAYS THE WAR HAS BEGUN**.

If war started, his mother, already a widow, would be frantic. And his sister. How old was she now? He must conclude his business today and leave tomorrow.

THE SAME MORNING

Mary Beth's foggy mind refused to work as she fingered the note in her hand. Easing herself down at her dressing table, she yawned, wondering who might need to communicate before seven in the morning. She had intended to sleep late after being up past midnight.

She tore open the note Maud had brought her.

Dearest Almost-Sister,

Did you see the flames on the mountain last night? The Aldehoff School celebrated the attack on Fort Sumter. Eddie said war has finally arrived. He and I are leaving hastily this morning so he can enlist. I knew you would want to hear from him since he intends to marry you. We will be truly sisters then. Pray for us.

Eileen

Mary Beth crumpled the note and threw it across the room. Eddie should have come to deliver his bad news— not sent word by his sister.

Would she ever see him again?

C&R Bank Office

The huge knot in Mary Beth's throat grew larger as she gazed at her father surrounded by file folders piled on and around his desk. She had never seen his office this messy. His gaunt face scowled as he made notes on a document. How long had he been working? She'd searched for him after reading Eileen's note, but Maud said her father had already left for work. "Papa, where is Fort Sumter?"

"Hello, dearie." Her father put down his pen and took a deep breath. "What smells so good? What did you bring in that basket?"

"Your breakfast." She deposited her offering on his desk and embraced him from behind. "I understand you skipped eating this morning."

"Cook's meal last night was filling." He caressed her cheek. "You are a blessing."

"Will you eat now, with me?"

"Of course." He stood. "Let's clear the desk. I've had Mr. Riddle reorganize a few files, and we are almost done."

Mary Beth plopped a stack of ledgers against the back wall beside her father's bookcase. "Is that why you came in early?"

"Oh, my office was much worse this morning." He pulled a chair closer and waved her to sit down at the cleared desk. "What do we have?"

Mary Beth pulled back the cloth to retrieve muffins and a bowl of jam, along with a small plate for each of them. At least she was getting him to eat. "Did you hear my question?"

A sheepish grin crossed his face. "I couldn't hear over my stomach. What was it?"

Mary Beth placed a muffin on each plate. "Fort Sumter.

I don't know where that is."

His eyebrows rose. "Oh. How did you—"

"Eddie's sister sent me a note this morning. Apparently, he chose to join up."

"I believe Fort Sumter is over three hundred miles from us. Trains can go up to thirty miles an hour. However, that's quite a long journey, my dear. But I truly hope cooler heads prevail." He patted her hand.

She placed a folded napkin by his plate. "Will Peter have any problems returning?"

"I hope not, but I think we should remember him as we thank God for this delightful breakfast." He reached for her hand.

Mary Beth bowed her head as her father prayed, hoping God would hear. Peter needed to come home.

May 1861
Wednesday
Fredericksburg, Virginia Train Station

Finally.

A sigh of relief escaped Peter's lips as he rose from the unrelenting hardness of the bench where he'd been sitting. Briefcase in hand, he followed the young Virginia militiaman who gestured at him. Maybe he'd be able to board a train for home soon.

Peter welcomed the fresh air after the odors of sweaty bodies and damp diapers coming from those that had arrived in Virginia with him. A second militiaman called others forward, too. Next to him, a lady hummed a lullaby to her sleeping baby, and a businessman, on his other side, carrying a portfolio, mumbled about the long wait. Peter's stomach churned as he thrust perspiring hands in his trouser pockets, fingering the letters from his family. No one had prepared him for a screening in the Confederacy. Would these papers see him through?

"In here." The soldier gestured through a wooden-framed doorway into a tiny windowless room. Peter stepped inside, catching his breath at the strong musty odor. The walls could use a coat of paint, but he didn't spot obvious mold. The room had no furniture except for a black metal desk with one straight and very uncomfortable-looking chair before it. On the other side of the desk, a hefty gray-haired soldier shuffled through a stack of papers sitting next to an ink stand.

"Sit down," the man said, without glancing up. He pulled a sheet of paper closer to him and reached for his pen. "What's your name and reason for entering the Confederacy?"

Peter lowered himself onto the chair and sat his briefcase in the floor. "I am Peter Allen Chandler. My father sent me on a European tour after I graduated from college, and I'm returning to Chattanooga, Tennessee, where I was born."

The bulky soldier gazed at him with narrowed eyes. "Europe, huh? How'd you return? What's your profession?"

"I landed in New York, and I'm a banker." Peter hesitated, deciding not to tell the soldier his briefcase contained an interest payment from one of their best clients. He *was* a banker, or at least he had the training, even though he'd never worked without supervision. What did the official need?

"Let's see your papers."

Peter pulled the letters out of his pocket, avoiding the

hated telegram, and offered them to the soldier.

The man held them to the light and examined them with a glass, as if Peter might be dangerous. He handed back the papers and glared at Peter with a frown. "I don't understand why a man of your age hasn't volunteered for military service."

"I've been out of the country." Peter knotted his right hand into a fist. Hadn't the man heard him the first time? An image of his grieving mother came to mind. He should not be wasting time here.

"Right. Europe. How nice." His face twisted into a sneer. "Were you unaware of what was happening here?" The soldier's voice rose. "We *mustn't* allow just anyone into Virginia. The Confederacy is at war." He drew out the word war in a low growl.

"I was in Italy when I received news of my father's death." Peter realized he'd been holding his breath and slowly let it out. What did this man hope to accomplish? "It took me several weeks to get passage here, and then I had to land in New York. I've been traveling since then attempting to return to my widowed mother."

"Indeed?" The man's eyebrows lowered. "And do you have proof of this?"

Peter ground his teeth, but he dug inside his pocket again. How he despised the telegram. "Here's the notice of my father's death. And here you can observe the date I boarded the ship that crossed the Atlantic. I have the receipt from the train I boarded to get here."

"Hmm." The militiaman studied the papers as though they might be counterfeit. "Since you came from overseas, it's going to require several hours to fill out the paperwork. However," He appraised Peter with narrowed black eyes "I could ask my superior officer for an emergency pass … for a certain fee." He jotted a number on paper and slid the note toward Peter.

Peter almost choked when he saw the sum and wished he hadn't mentioned he was a banker, but he refused to lie. His anxiety gave way to rising indignation. "That's unacceptable."

"Very well." The soldier shrugged and then stood. "I shall attempt to persuade Major Jones anyhow." He turned and left the room.

Now what? Peter's heart pounded. Should he have paid—?

Suddenly, the door flew open.

Peter jerked at the sound, snatching his briefcase.

Two soldiers pushed in, grabbed Peter's arms and, before he could protest, shoved him down the hall and into a small dirty room.

The lock clicked behind them as they left.

Later That Evening
Prayer Meeting
First Presbyterian Church

The sweet smell of flowers surrounded Mary Beth as she entered the foyer of the church where an arrangement of lilies stood. Clusters of people dressed in their best hovered in small groups while her father escorted her like a princess. She smiled up into his handsome ruddy face, and he grinned in return, his green eyes radiated his adoration. If only his face was less care-worn. "You look so tired, Papa."

"We are in the Lord's house, dearie. Besides, I'm always tired after work." He winked.

A sound to the right caught Mary Beth's attention, and she turned to see Jane Haskell, one of her best friends. She had her brown hair pulled up in a fashionable chignon, but her brown eyes held a look of concern.

"Papa. I must speak to Jane. See? She appears distressed."

Her father patted her hand. "I *do* see. But remember, do not assume the worst until you know the truth."

Dearest Papa. While yet a baby, she'd lost her mother, but her father's affection had kept her secure.

"I shall be ..." He pointed to the sanctuary and dropped a kiss on her cheek before ambling into the auditorium.

She hurried to her friend as the organ in the next room began a prelude. "Jane, is something amiss?"

"It's Fred. The military reported he is ... ill." Jane pulled a delicate handkerchief from her drawstring bag and blotted her nose.

"Dreadful." A graduate of West Point, Fred had lived with the Haskell family after his father's death. Mary Beth engulfed her friend in a quick hug. "How dreary. I can't believe you came."

"Father insisted." Several tears streaked down her cheeks. "Guess I need prayer, though."

Mary Beth held her friend's hand and tried to think of comforting words. None of the lovely phrases her elders repeated seemed adequate. Plus, she worried about Eddie since he'd joined the military. She would never understand why men longed to face battle and the possibility of death. Caution seemed much wiser.

Jeanie, an acquaintance from across town, rushed into

the foyer, her face flushed and black hair mussed from running. She grabbed Mary Beth's arm. "Eddie. He's gone."

Mary Beth dropped Jane's hands and turned to Jeanie. Of course, Eddie was gone. Her pronouncement made no sense. "What?"

"He's dead." She wiped sweat from her face. "Gone forever."

The room faded as Mary Beth tried to imagine how that could be. His banter and jokes could entertain her for hours. Eddie had radiated energy, life, and confidence. How could he be dead?

Peter sneezed several times and pulled thin, silky strands off his face. Apparently when the militiamen deposited him in this tiny room, they had disturbed a few cobwebs. The stale odor made him gag. His eyes finally adjusted to the darkness, and he tried to turn the doorknob. Locked. The only light came from under the door, but he had enough to examine his surroundings. The room had peeling paint, a dirty hardwood floor, and indentations on the walls where shelves appeared to have been. The soldiers had secured Peter in a closet.

Mr. Roper was doing all the banking without him. If only he could go home and share the burden.

He pulled out his pocketknife and inserted the blade into the lock, but it was too short to turn the tumblers. If only he had a smaller tool, thin enough to insert further in. Running his fingers under the door, he could tell the door measured about two inches thick, almost impossible to break down. Nevertheless, he threw his weight against the door until he was breathless. If he could get a running start, the door latch might give, but the room was too small.

Panting, Peter squatted in the corner of the room, knowing his clothes would be filthy when someone rescued him. He hated that, but he couldn't stand for hours. Shouting might work, but he doubted anyone would listen. His mother should have received his tentative travel schedule and would worry when she received no more telegrams. He bowed his head and petitioned God for safety and rescue.

Several hours passed, and Peter felt light-headed. Did this room have enough air to sustain him? He sent another prayer heavenward.

A clanging sound caught Peter's attention, and he rose from the wooden floor, brushing off his clothes. The clanging grew closer until metal grated upon metal, and the lock clicked. Light flooded the room. Peter could barely see the elderly man who opened the door, but he was not dressed in a uniform. A huge ring of keys dangled from his hand. "I hope you came to release me."

"I am the station master. The militia's gone home." The man released a dry cough. "Everyone worries about spies these days. By rail, we aren't that far from Washington, you know."

"I can assure you. I am no spy." Being confused for a spy made Peter's stomach turn.

"No, sir." The elderly man shook his head. "Per telegram. The last train is about to leave. I thought I'd best let you go."

"Telegram?" Peter could see better now, and the

scrubby man before him wore a long-sleeved shirt, vest, and a billed cap like the man who sold train tickets. "You verified my identity?"

"Indeed. You are fortunate. Our telegraph worked." The man cackled. "The Chattanooga mayor vouches for you. Them militiamen are trying to fund the new government, you know—or else line their pockets. Now hurry."

Peter rushed to the train.

CHAPTER TWO

MARY BETH'S BEDROOM

Mary Beth sat at her mahogany dressing table, gazing in the mirror at her chubby Negro companion and former nurse standing behind her. She enjoyed the feel of the bristles caressing her scalp as Elsie brushed out her long, blonde hair. Mary Beth needed Elsie's assistance with a new hairstyle she had seen at church. She wanted her hair fixed before she ran down to the train depot. They usually posted military casualties late in the day, and she would make sure Eddie's name wasn't there. Jeanie could not be correct. She hardly knew him.

"You best be a tellin' me what you want. My arms be a gettin' tired."

"Braid the hair on each side and bring it up to attach to the bun in the back." Mary Beth pulled back a lock of hair on one side to demonstrate the drape. "It should look like this."

"That means you be lookin' forward the entire time." Elsie gathered up bits of hair by Mary Beth's face and brushed it out.

"I shall. Please braid." Holding still, she let her gaze roam the mahogany frame around the oval of the mirror before her. As a child, she imagined the trio of engraved roses at the top represented the three in her family—Elsie, who filled in for her mother, her father, and herself. Further down, one engraved rose embellished each side. The rose on the right stood for Mary Beth, and the left for her father. "That's tight."

"Ya moved." Elsie's dark hands dropped the braid. "Tis ruined."

"Start over. Please." Mary Beth loosened the braid and spun around to look into Elsie's brown eyes. "I promise to be still."

"If ya wish ..."

She settled herself facing forward at the mirror again, staring at her face, her blonde hair, and roses on the mirror. She tried not to think about Jeannie's terrible announcement yesterday.

Bang! A commotion came from the room beneath them, her father's library.

Mary Beth jumped, pulling her hair away from Elsie's tight grip. "Ouch. What was that?"

"I be thinkin' something big be fallin' in the library." Elsie picked up the brush and combed out the braid.

Loud voices reverberated through the floor.

"That's not my father, is it?" Mary Beth looked at Elsie's reflection.

"No." Elsie tilted her head as the voices continued. "But that ... might be."

Mary Beth rushed for the door. A hairstyle that required her to be still so long might not be worth the effort. "Let's braid later."

Mary Beth's hair swished around her shoulders as she

dashed out of her bedroom and ran down the thickly carpeted stairs. Her father never raised his voice. However, as she reached the foyer, Jeanie's father, Mr. Winter, stalked past. His reddened face twisted into a scowl, he collided with the huge palm that sat by the door, knocking the plant to the ground as he dashed out of the house. Dirt scattered across the floor.

"Mr. Winter?" Mary Beth hurried to the plant and almost struck Maud as she ran in from the kitchen. "What came over him?"

Maud shook her head and placed both hands on her hips. "Well, I never. That man bein' angrier than a growlin' dog. He be actin' like Satan's own and what a mess he be a makin.' Be assured, I will see to this here mess. Mr. Roper, fine man that he is, would never be a makin' all that noise."

"Thank you, Maud." Even though she was freed from slavery, Maud had chosen to stay on as a paid servant, as Elsie had done. Longing to discover the cause of the shouting, Mary Beth rushed to the library at end of the hall. The door stood ajar, and she pushed in to discover a peaceful scene—her father, reading glasses perched on his face, occupied the chair by the desk reading as if nothing happened. The bookshelves behind him remained untouched. The scent of cinnamon and sugar filled the air. "What smells so good? I heard shouting."

Her father put down the paper and pointed to a plate of rolls and a pot of tea. "I asked Cook for some pastries, hoping to calm Mr. Winter. I guess you could tell the delicacies failed to work their usual magic."

"Yesterday, Jeanie announced bad news about a person named Eddie." Mary Beth cut herself a slice of pastry and took a tiny bite. She had not mentioned Jeannie's proclamation to her father because subjects that upset her were hard to talk about. However, now that Mr. Winter had visited, her stomach ached.

Her father nodded. "I am sorry to say I have seen many dishonest people in this world. It's too easy to live selfishly rather than valuing truth."

"Who is the man she refers to?" The sight of the pastry in her hand nauseated her. "Jeannie did *not* know my Eddie."

"I am sorry to say she did." Her father stood and put his arm around her shoulders "It appears Eddie had asked for Jeanie's hand."

"What?" Tears sprang to her eyes, and she put down the unfinished pastry. "That cannot be true. He was courting me."

Her father kissed the top of her head. "I know he appeared to be, but Mr. Winter said Eddie asked to marry her before he left town for the army."

Mary Beth covered her face as tears escaped down her cheeks. Her father's arms engulfed her, and she buried herself in the warmth of his shirt.

Mary Beth attempted to set aside her sadness as she entered the dining room. Her father sprang to his feet to help her with her chair. The aroma of fried chicken and mashed potatoes engulfed her as she took her place at the table. After scooting up her chair, her father sat across from her. Maud had laid out the fine china, which had belonged to her mother. Mary Beth had always loved the intertwined pink flowers around the rim. She picked up the lace napkin by her plate and gazed at her father. Had anyone ever loved a daughter more? In light of the bad news, her appetite had not returned, but she would do her best to honor him. "Did you ask Maud to use our best?"

"I did." He glowed. "We must celebrate you tonight. I was … unwilling to let Eddie have you. Now I celebrate because I do not have to."

A giggle escaped her lips, surprising her. She should be grieving.

"He was not good enough."

Her face grew warm as laughter bubbled up. Once again, her father's kindness overcame her sadness. "While I was dressing, it occurred to me … why did Mr. Winter come? He did not come about … Eddie. Did he?"

"No." He piled potatoes on his plate and did not look up.

She must know, but her father's mouth tightened. "Please, Father."

"During dinner, we should speak of more pleasant matters." He reached for the chicken. "Would you like some?"

A persistent knock rattled the front door.

Mary Beth's father glanced toward the dining room door leading into the foyer. "I'm glad that door is closed."

Bang. Bang, Bang. "Roper! You must listen to my concerns."

"Is that the grocer?" Mary Beth put down the plate her father had handed her. She'd seen Mr. Nelson drunk before.

Her father took a sip of his tea. "This is excellent. We will have to commend the cook. Remind me, please."

Mary Beth glared at him. Praising tea at a moment like

this? Something had happened in the city, and her father didn't want her to know. Now that she had come of age, he shouldn't be hiding information from her. But what could she do?

"I will not be ignored." The voice grew louder. "I tried at the bank."

Her father grimaced and pushed back his chair. "That's Mr. Nelson, and I think he came inside. How rude."

Wearing a soiled white apron and a sweat soaked shirt beneath, Nelson rushed into the dining room, breathing hard. "Men are coming—"

Maud ran in behind him, wringing her hands. "I be a tellin' him no. I done said he cannot come in. But he pushin' right past me, Mr. Roper, sir. So sorry, sir."

"Never mind, Maud. I will deal with this." Her father grabbed the intruder and led him out of the room through the door he had entered. "Mr. Nelson, my daughter and I are eating."

"Terribly sorry. Mr. Nelson be shovin' past me." Maud fled through the opposite door to the kitchen.

Mary Beth grabbed tea and took a gulp to unclog her tight throat.

"Everyone is furious," the unwanted visitor bellowed.

Mary Beth's heart pounded, and she pushed aside her plate. Was the city in danger? She tiptoed to the door and looked into the foyer. They must be heading for the library rather than the sitting room. She moved down the hall without making a sound. If they closed the door, she could listen outside.

"Seventy-five thousand troops ... shooting our boys," Nelson said. "That's not freedom."

The library door closed with a click, muffling their

voices. Mary Beth slipped further down the hall, listening.

"Your bank won't be safe," Nelson bellowed. "Lincoln is a tyrant ... troops ..."

Mary Beth's stomach churned. Losing Eddie had upset her, but what if Mr. Nelson was correct? If the bank was in danger, Papa must act. However, she still couldn't hear everything. Maybe if she put her ear on the door.

She eased closer, holding her skirt still so it wouldn't crinkle.

"Tennessee should secede to protect states' rights," Nelson yelled.

"... wise ... act without thinking," her father said.

More banging thundered on the front door again, and Mary Beth eased away from the library, tiptoeing down the hall. The sound of men shouting alarmed her as she neared the door. Was every man in the city upset?

Maud came scampering into the hall and almost collided with Mary Beth.

"Huh! Miss Roper?" Maud put her hand on her chest. "Whew. You done scared me, sneakin' around like that."

Maud kept talking, but Mary Beth darted past her and ran upstairs to her bedroom. What if Maud told her father she was 'sneaking' down the hallway? Her father wouldn't be pleased she'd listened at the door, yet the city faced a threat. She much preferred to know the bad news.

CHAPTER THREE

JUNE 1861

The train whistle announced its arrival at Lynchburg, Virginia. Peter sighed with relief. He had seen tobacco fields and warehouses from his window and knew they must be close to the city. His muscles ached from sitting, and he hadn't slept in days. Fortunately, he had planned to meet a college friend here. He hoped for a day of rest and a first-hand update on politics. The fiasco he experienced entering Virginia worried him. What if he was given the same treatment here as well?

Soldiers dressed in a variety of uniforms mingled with the people who strolled around on the platform outside the large brick depot. A porter, dressed in blue, rushed into the car and clapped his hands. When the travelers stopped moving and talking, he spoke, "You must all disembark. End of the line for this train."

A man stood and yelled, "Why does the line end here?"

"Repairs to the track. Make other arrangements at the ticket counter." The porter waved toward the depot and left the car.

No. Peter grew hot. Why didn't train personnel tell them earlier? The bank's welfare loomed in his thoughts. How was Mr. Roper handling the extra work? Perhaps the tracks couldn't handle the extra traffic the war was bringing.

The lady who sat in front of Peter dropped her jacket, and he leaned forward to retrieve it for her. He waved several more ladies and a young family past. When the car had almost emptied, he fetched his trunk and portfolio from the overhead rack.

The odor of tobacco hung in the air as Peter dragged his luggage onto the platform. What a relief to spot his friend. Bob Reynolds stood taller than most men and had blond hair, almost fuzzy with curl. Peter put down his trunk to wave. Bob rushed toward him, dodging travelers and luggage. "Peter. You look tired. My servant will transport your luggage to my house. There's a fine restaurant down the road where we can eat."

"You received my telegram. I heard they don't always arrive." Peter tapped his friend on the shoulder. "How are you?"

"Much better than you appear. You must be exhausted." Bob nodded to a heavy-set Negro behind him, who grabbed the trunk.

"Officials closed the rail line. Do you know about that?" Peter waved toward the train he just left.

Bob nodded. "War. Tracks are being destroyed. Plus, Colonel Jackson just stole engines from the Ohio railroad. He's moving them into the South for the newly forming nation. The military gets priority seating. You may have to stay a few days."

Peter groaned and explained his need to complete his trip.

"Maybe you could rent a coach, but that's become dangerous," Bob said. "You could get caught in a battle."

Bob navigated Peter through the crowded depot and onto a wooden sidewalk along a wide dirt road filled with carriages and buggies. Stores and merchants lined the sidewalk. Peter turned to his friend, relating his adventure entering the Confederacy. "What changed?"

"Everything." Bob shook his head. "The frenzy over slavery—exploded. Now we have a spy network. They are alert for anyone who might give information to the Union. Virginia seceded when Lincoln raised troops."

"I never thought this controversy would lead to war." Peter wondered how this change would impact banking.

HASKELL'S GARDEN

Bright sunshine warmed Mary Beth's skin while she stood among the rose bushes behind the Haskell's home. She gazed at the white rose, and then the yellow rose Jane's mother pointed out. How exquisite. However, beauty failed to penetrate her soul. She had come to chat with Jane about her worries, but Mrs. Haskell took her to the garden to see the roses. Did she say Jane was coming? A swishing noise made her look toward the fine brick house adorned with white shutters, but a gray rabbit hopped through the grass, not her friend. Mrs. Haskell kept talking, but Mary Beth missed most of it. She bent her nose down toward the stunning red rose Mrs. Haskell held for her. A tiny drop of water quivered on one petal. "M-m-m-m. That smells wonderful. You were saying—"

"My friend attended the first Royal Horticultural Society Rose show in 1858. London. Can you imagine? Spectacular, of course." Mrs. Haskell closed her eyes and tilted her head. The sun glinted on her light brown hair.

"Excellent." London would be safer than her hometown right now.

"Someday, I plan to attend. I am sure Mr. Haskell will agree." She waved her arm over all the rose bushes. "All of these are gifts."

"Really?" Mary Beth counted the rose bushes. "You must have eight."

"Ten." Mrs. Haskell pointed out two small bushes, hidden by taller ones. "These are new. No blooms yet."

"Had you always had this area cultivated before you added roses?" Mary Beth admired the well-trimmed shrubs, interspersed with clusters of daisies.

"Mary Beth?"

Mary Beth almost jumped at the sound of her name. Dabbing at her face with a handkerchief, Jane ambled toward her from a thicket, her eyes slightly reddened. "Jane. How are you?"

"I was taking the air and praying." She nodded toward the woods behind the garden. "It always helps me feel better."

"Indeed." Her mother's face glowed as she smiled at her daughter. "Fine medicine for the soul. But let me answer your question."

Mary Beth had forgotten the conversation. "Question?"

Mrs. Haskell smiled. "We were working on this area to plant a garden when Celeste gave me the first bush."

"How fortunate. You could integrate the roses in more easily." She turned to Jane. "I hesitate to ask, but I wonder if you have news about Fred?"

Jane closed her eyes and covered her mouth. "A putrid fever. That's all we know."

"Oh. Somehow, I thought he might be improved.

Surely you will hear something if—"

"No," Jane said. "We've been told they can't send bodies home."

"But remember, we have no reason to believe he might be dead." Mrs. Haskell patted Jane's shoulder.

Mary Beth coughed several times, unsure what to say. She hadn't intended to ask what would happen if he died.

Mrs. Haskell patted her back. "I should send for tea."

"Thank you." Alone with Jane at last. As Jane's mother walked away, Mary Beth told about Mr. Nelson and Mr. Winter. "Is Chattanooga in danger?"

"Most people are upset," Jane said.

"Why? States have seceded, but they formed their own country."

"After Confederate soldiers fired on Ft. Sumter, Lincoln said he would raise seventy-five thousand troops. Everyone in Chattanooga is furious he would start a war."

Mary Beth held her breath. "Forcing them to return?"

"Yes." Jane swallowed. "You see, South Carolina asked the Union to leave Fort Sumter, but they didn't. That's why they attacked."

"The Union fought back." Mary Beth heard her father talking to men at church about that, but she did not see the significance.

"Chattanooga will vote whether or not to leave the Union. Soon."

And if we do? Now that Mary Beth knew the latest, she did not want to think about what might happen.

The next day, Peter had to navigate through a crowd of

sweaty men who filled the depot. Some wore ragged militia uniforms and others wore varying colors. He walked up to a man wearing a navy dress uniform and carrying a rifle. "Where's the end of the line?"

The man pointed toward the opposite wall. "There. It winds around the inside. Are you joining up?"

"I must return to Tennessee first. Widowed mother."

"Oh. Sorry." The man's eyes softened. "Rail lines aren't intact in that direction."

Peter's heart sank as he envisioned his mother's anxiety. Bob had asked around amongst his friends but found no one who would undertake the trip. "You know anyone with a carriage who could take me?"

"No." The young man's face darkened. "You might buy a horse, if you could find someone willing to sell."

"What's going on here?" Peter eyed the men around him who looked prepared to fight.

"Signing up to fight." He pointed to the ticket window. "We are getting tickets to Richmond."

"Any chance the tracks will be repaired soon? I must go toward Tennessee?"

"No, sir." The man kicked a pebble. "You'd best come with us. My pa works for the railroad. He said those tracks will take months to repair."

Would Peter's mother worry?

CHAPTER FOUR

7 JUNE 1861

As if unaware of the danger, the sun glowed in the sky surrounded by fluffy clouds as Mary Beth and her father descended the steps of their home. She hung onto her father's arm as they strolled down the gravel walkway lined with flowers. A drawstring purse hung on her right arm as she held her fan. June in Tennessee delivered muggy, hot weather one must prepare for. After talking to Jane, she had a better grasp of the situation, but she needed to understand the whole problem. She and her father turned left on the dirt road, and she looked forward to the shaded area where huge trees grew up ahead. "Papa, tell me about the meeting we are attending."

"The Crutchfield House has a large meeting room."

"Yes, I understand hotels often do." She replied as she fanned her face.

"Chattanoogans planned a meeting to discuss the good and bad points of joining the Confederacy."

"Good points?"

"Yes." He smiled down at her and his green eyes sparkled. "Should states be free to leave the Union? Freedom is the subject."

Anytime he smiled like that, she relaxed. Today the muscles in her face and jaw grew tighter. "But if the Union attacks us …"

"We would have to win."

She glanced around at familiar sights around her—the trees, shrubs, and even the rocks beside the road. Yet, the unfamiliar and unpleasant might await her. "Why? I don't understand. Slavery? Isn't it wrong?"

"That is the dilemma, Mary Beth." He sighed and glanced down at her. "At times in life, we must choose between two options we don't like."

He wasn't making sense. "You are saying—"

"Slavery should end, so I agree with the Union. However, must they force themselves on us?"

"Easy. If we stay in the Union, we avoid war," Mary Beth said. That seemed the most appropriate. Every citizen should agree to avoid bloodshed.

"Not necessarily." Her father pressed his lips into a thin line.

"What?"

"It's likely our boys will be shooting either way. The North is calling for soldiers."

Mary Beth exhaled. A bird fluttered past, and she imagined her hope leaving the same way. She had asked for him to explain. Understanding should remove fear, but her whole body tensed anyway.

He patted her left hand, in the crook of his arm. "I preferred to keep this from you."

No. She could be strong if she had to be. Later. Maybe the two countries would settle their differences another way. Today, she would enjoy observing what the ladies wore.

They neared the city where stores had put up closed signs, and people walked the same direction. Mary Beth had only seen Crutchfield House from the outside. The three-story brick building sat across from the railroad. The old house boasted a full-length porch along the front of each floor. Her father opened the door, and she inhaled in awe. Tall white columns supported a high ceiling. Walnut paneling covered the walls, and the floor had plush red carpet.

Her father ambled to the marble counter where a uniformed man sat. "We are here for the meeting."

The man nodded. "The hallway to your left takes you to the ballroom. Follow it all the way to the back."

Such luxury. Mary Beth imagined she was royalty, and she glided like a queen. At last, she waltzed into the assembly room where glass chandeliers spread dappled light. Maple bow-back chairs with cane seats sat in rows with an aisle down the middle facing a huge carved lectern opposite the door. However, people filled almost every seat.

The Malone family sat in the back with all six of their children, and across the aisle Fred and Wanda Peters sat with their arms crossed. Jane Haskell stood near the front of the room waving. Mary Beth smiled and waved back. "Papa, I think the Haskells saved us a place up front."

"Then we'd best hurry up there. I did not realize the building would be so packed."

A shiver sizzled up Mary Beth's spine as she walked toward her friend. Mumblings around her didn't sound friendly, and she hoped nothing unpleasant happened. But at least she would not have to rely on hearsay tomorrow when friends dropped by.

Mary Beth reached the row of wooden chairs where Jane stood, and they scooted past the family to sit in the middle of the row. "Papa, will this take long?"

"I did not think so," he said glancing around. "But I believe we might have some angry citizens here."

The mayor, who wore a navy suit, hovered at the front of the room. At last, he stepped up to the lectern and accepted a gavel from a man dressed in a hotel uniform. He banged the lectern. "We have a speaker for tonight. Once he talks, we will allow anyone to give their opinion. Of course, we want to be fair and allow anyone to participate who wants to. Fred Hood, editor of the *Gazette*, will speak."

"No. He made known his position." A man shouted from the back.

"Quiet, please." The mayor banged his gavel again. "We will hear from *anyone* who wants to speak."

Hood approached the lectern, and ran his hands along the its sides. "Chattanooga residents will not enjoy being enslaved by the Confederate army. If you want marital law, leave the Union."

A man stood and waved his gun. "We want to hear from someone else."

Men began to shout, and Mary Beth could not differentiate their voices.

Hood walked away, and the mayor's face reddened as he banged the gavel. "One at a time. Otherwise you cannot be heard."

A dark-headed man stood. "We want a just government, and at this point, our northern citizens have destroyed our Constitutional freedoms."

"That's right."

"I do not agree."

Shouting filled the room again.

"We must stand up for our rights," a man shouted from the other side of the room. "Or else we will lose our freedom."

"And what of the Negro? Do we judge him to be less human than ourselves?" Another man yelled.

"Boo."

Clusters of people left the room.

The mayor waved his gavel. "With the election coming up, tomorrow our city must decide whether to stay in the Union or secede. I thought talking over the issues would be healthy."

More booing.

Mary Beth's heart quickened. How violent would the people be if the mayor insisted?

Mr. Hill, editor of the *Advertiser* stood up. "We have no cause to break up the Union. Chattanooga is our home, and we want to live in peace."

Several men stood to their feet and yelled at each other. Other men pulled out guns.

The mayor frowned and shouted, but Mary Beth could not hear him.

A farmer wearing faded overalls stood. "I have no plans to vote for anything Hood would recommend. We are citizens of Tennessee first and of the United States second. Anyone who says different represents a hostile power at war with us."

The shoemaker rose to his feet. "I agree. I want to hear from the editor of the other paper."

A man wearing a dark suit hopped up. "We can vote without arguing."

More than half the room stood and cheered.

Mary Beth leaned closer to her father, wishing she could slip out the back. The angry voices unsettled her, and she hoped they did not come to blows. What was happening to her peaceful hometown?

10 JUNE 1861
EARLY EVENING
ROPER DINING ROOM

Mary Beth inhaled the fragrance of the warm tea as she poured a cup for her father and passed the beverage across the dining table to him. They had just finished a light dinner, and Maud had brought cinnamon rolls after clearing away dirty dishes. Her father's face had more lines, and he sat slumped over, rubbing his eyes. She hoped tea and rest restored his energies. The dear man worked too hard. If only Peter Chandler arrived before Papa ruined his health entirely. She looked forward to a lively chat about his day at the bank. "I asked Cook to steep the tea longer tonight, and I added extra sugar."

"You are sweet enough for me." He patted her hand and smiled.

Maud, their housekeeper, knocked at the open door and bustled in waving a piece of paper. "Mr. Roper be gettin' a message and I knowed he be a wantin' to read the election numbers. And I done bring this message right now. Knowin' you be pleased."

"Your efficiency blesses us daily." He held out his hand for the note.

"Oh, sir. If any be blessed, 'tis me. Workin' for a man so fine—"

"Good work, Maud. You may go." Mr. Roper opened the note and gazed at its contents.

Maud closed her mouth and left.

"Statewide results?" Mary Beth sat forward, trying to see the writing.

He nodded, tightening his lips. "Maud was correct. Votes are in. Tennessee will leave the Union."

"What?" Mary Beth gasped. Chattanooga had voted to remain in the Union. She had hoped and prayed the rest of the state would agree. The Bible said God answered prayer. Why didn't he? Wasn't he listening? "No. I thought you heard … that cannot be right. What happened?"

"The western portions of the state … voted differently." Mr. Roper put aside the letter and gulped his tea.

Her father's grave expression alarmed her. "How…will this affect us?"

Papa patted her hand. "Are you sure you want to know?"

Mary Beth inhaled against tightness in her chest. She was no longer a child and could not bear to be left out of the danger. "I want to … need to understand."

Her father smiled and sat back in his chair. "The news is bad, but we face no immediate danger."

"Then tell me," she pleaded. Her heart rate sped up with the images of cannons and gunfire.

"Lincoln has chosen to make the Federal government stronger than the state by raising an army. If the army shoots at us, we must defend ourselves. We are caught in a situation beyond our control. I do not like this."

She ran a hand over her mouth, nodding.

Her father dumped another spoon of sugar in his tea. "There are good points in favor of the South."

"Go on." Mary Beth held her breath. Her father never overstated the problem.

"We have good generals, better than the North, and we should be able to protect ourselves."

"And?" She had to know the worst, even though she would hate herself for asking in the next moment.

"We have fewer people and less machinery to produce weaponry, which goes against us."

"Could we see fighting here?"

"Maybe."

War. She could lose her home, her father, her life.

CHAPTER FIVE

15 JUNE 1861
NOON

Peter took a deep breath as the train pulled to a halt in the Chattanooga station, puffing and hissing steam. Home at last! He gazed out the window at the brick depot with arched windows and spotted his mother, dressed in a black dress and hat, standing on the platform twisting a white handkerchief. Beside her stood a young lady with light brown hair who must be his sister, Ruth. She had grown much taller, and he almost did not recognize her. His father, however, was not there. He swallowed to hold back tears.

Peter rose, reached overhead to get his bag, and eased into the aisle with the other travelers. A lump formed in his throat. What would he say to his widowed mother?

At last, he jumped down from the train onto the crowded wooden platform to be immediately embraced by his weeping mother. Her reddened eyes distressed him.

"Peter." She pulled away and cupped his face. "How your father would love to be here."

"Petie!" Ruth squealed out her pet name for him and squeezed between him and his mother. "I missed you."

Tears dampened his cheeks as he pressed his sister into a hug. He had wanted this moment for months. Now that he stood here on the platform swarming with people, he couldn't articulate comforting words. Death had robbed him of his father and reversed his role from child to protector. Unthinkable! What a spectacle they made for the busy travelers.

His mother took his hand. "You will want to visit the grave, so I brought the carriage."

This wasn't the homecoming he expected, but he could not refuse Mama. She had grown smaller, more vulnerable, and he would not cause her pain.

Could he be strong enough for the two ladies in his life?

Peter was thankful Citizen's Cemetery had tall, thick trees to protect them from the heat of the blazing June sun. Sweat trickled down his back as he opened the black wrought iron gate for his mother and ambled with her through the grass-filled plot. What a lovely walk, except for gray and white stones dotting the landscape—a reminder of loved ones now passed.

"Just over there." His mother pointed. "We only ... erected a wooden cross. For now."

Peter understood. She had waited until he came home. He followed her to the spot. Dried dirt covered the oblong bit of land before him, like a huge scar amongst the green, reminding him of the freshness of his grief. His mother clung to him, weeping, and tears streaked his own face. He came here to learn the whole story, to let his mother cry, to grieve for the father he admired. "Tell me ... how you heard."

His mother hiccupped and sighed. "I was expecting ... a telegram. Your father ... always let me know he was safe. He had never visited that particular bank. It was in ...

Alabama. New client, you see."

Peter would ask Mr. Roper if the bank needed another visit. He sighed as her tears flowed anew. "Train accident?"

She sniffled. "No. Bits of the track … came loose from their fittings … crashing into the train car."

Northern train systems outstripped the South in safety and efficiency, but the facts would not help his mother grieve.

She blotted her face with her handkerchief. "I did not hear … for several days … I worried."

A footstep behind Peter caught his attention, and he turned to see their butler, Billy. A tall, muscular Negro, Billy stood back from the grave holding a slip of paper in his hand.

"Did you need me?"

"Sir, a message be comin' for you from Mr. Roper, and I thought you might be needin' to know the information."

Peter took the paper Billy extended. "Very good. You have done well."

"Will ya be wantin' to answer, sir?" He shuffled his feet. "I can be waitin' if ya do."

Peter opened the message and read.

Peter,

Thanks for informing me of your arrival today. Welcome home.

My condolences on the death of your father.

We have an immediate problem to discuss regarding the bank. Please drop by my home as soon as you can.

Mr. Roper

Peter did not want to face banking problems today, and he could not imagine what was so important. However, his bank partner, Mr. Roper, did not give alarms unnecessarily. "Please inform Mr. Roper I shall visit him shortly."

Billy nodded and left.

Peter stood with his mother and shared favorite memories for another hour.

"I am tired." Peter's mother stepped away from him and placed her hand on the wooden cross marking the grave. "Please accompany me home before you see Mr. Roper."

"Of course." Peter guided his mother out of the graveyard and into the carriage. His fondest dream had been working alongside his father. Despite the June sunshine, shadows engulfed Peter as he contemplated banking without his father.

Peter strode down Main Street on his way to the Roper home, his mind occupied with the responsibility he now carried. The clicking of his feet on the wooden sidewalk made a hollow sound, as if life had no meaning. A man lived for a few years, maybe sixty. Then he died. His job became the duty of another person. How dreary.

Life brought pain. His mother's face came to mind. She had burst into violent weeping as Peter left her in the sitting room moments ago. What crisis had overtaken the bank that his partner would need to talk to him the day he arrived?

He passed the bakery and the dry goods store and wondered about the cluster of men on the far corner. The voices sounded sharp, maybe angry, and he had to pass them.

"… no one says that … No."

"Liar!"

"Answer me."

"I won't."

Wham!

That sound of flesh and bone crashing together made Peter ill.

"I will shoot …"

Indistinct shouting.

A fight. More people gathered. Peter crossed the street to get away from the crowd. He stepped into the road just as a man riding a horse galloped past in a whirl of dust. The man stopped at the crowd too.

More shouting.

I am taking the long way around.

ROPER HOME

Mary Beth caught her breath when she heard a knock on the front door. Peter had arrived. Maud was off tonight, so she ran to the door to find him serious and quiet. Her cheeks burned. How should she greet her childhood friend? When they grew up together, she had no qualms about teasing him. Her relationship with Eddie had changed all that. Her gaze wandered to his eyes for a second, hoping he had forgiven her. "Hello, Peter."

"Hello. Your father … wanted to see me?"

Brief. What else could she expect? She stepped away

from the door and looked at the floor. "Yes. Go to the library. I shall fetch pastries right from the oven."

"I would like that. How have you been?"

"Good." She had no intention of telling him of her anxiety. Instead, she nodded toward the library. "Make yourself at home."

Peter turned as Mary Beth fled to the kitchen where cook was opening the stove and removing a pan of hot gingerbread cookies.

"My lands, child. You bein' sick?" Bessie, the plump Negro cook, frowned as she put the pan down on top of the woodstove. "You be too white."

Mary Beth snatched a warm cookie, allowing the sweetness to dissolve in her mouth. "I am just hungry for your baking, and I need refreshments for Papa and Peter."

"I be thinkin' that boy be sad comin' home to his widowed ma." Bessie reached into the cabinet for a platter. "You be givin' him several cookies. Hear?"

She snatched the goodies cook offered and gathered napkins and iced tea. If only she could pretend nothing was wrong when she served Peter.

As Peter entered the Chandler library, Mr. Roper rose from his large desk and extended his hand. He had more gray hair and had added a slight paunch. "Hello, Peter. I would like to introduce you to Mr. Edward Harden. He gave me information I wanted you to hear."

A thin man with short auburn-brown hair stood and smiled. "I heard so much about you from your father. I was sorry to hear about his accident."

Peter cleared his throat to hold back emotion. His father should be making this introduction instead of Roper. "We were close."

"And I am sure you have his excellent character," Mr. Harden said.

Peter swallowed hard.

"Please sit down, Peter," Roper said. He waved to a wing chair beside Mr. Harden. "I asked Edward here today to share his experience with his neighbor, Mr. Henry Carter."

Harden nodded. "His property borders mine, and I know he invested most of his money in a California gold mine that failed. His situation must be terrible. He used to ask me for food, and so I allowed him to take my chickens on occasion to prevent him from going hungry."

"So compassionate." Roper tapped the arm of his chair. "Go on, Edward. You have more."

"Carter said he was behind on his mortgage, but I refused to give him money. I also overheard him talking about leaving town to avoid debt. So, I thought it best to report to you." Mr. Harden rose and walked toward the door. "Should you foreclose, I am willing to buy the property. Of course, you may have other options."

Roper hopped up and walked him toward the door. "I appreciate the news."

Once Edward Harden left, Mr. Roper returned to his chair. "Such a sad situation. Mr. Carter valued all the wrong things, causing him to suffer and impacting his neighbors."

"Is this the reason you asked to speak to me tonight?"

"Yes," Roper pulled up the chair Harden vacated. "I apologize for plunging you into work. You have only arrived ... and your family. Terribly sad. However, we have two pressing issues. Carter's loan, which is long overdue."

Peter nodded. "And the second issue?"

"Tennessee voted to leave the Union. Usually the sheriff and I serve the papers when I foreclose and take possession. However, Eastern Tennessee did not want to join the Confederacy. I heard there's an outcry to stay in the Union ... as a separate state. Maybe rioting. Our citizens are ... uneasy. I doubt the sheriff can accompany us."

"That explains ..." Peter told what he saw on the way. He now understood Roper's concerns. And that explained why entering Tennessee by train had not been a problem. He had expected to be grilled again as he entered the Union. "How complicated."

"Indeed. People in our city reach for their firearms when such topics arise." Roper rubbed his hands together. "I fear we may have to do this together tomorrow."

Peter pushed back his chair and stood. "I shall locate my father's rifle tonight."

"Get a gun you can conceal. That might work better." Mr. Roper raised an eyebrow. "But I am afraid we are not finished yet."

"Oh." Peter eased back down. He was acting like a college freshman and he hated his inexperience.

"The transition from the Union to the Confederacy will create chaos at the bank. We'd best discuss how we will accept payments."

Peter rubbed his forehead and prayed he would be adequate for this job.

Mary Beth carried a tray of cookies into her father's

library, but she dreaded looking at Peter's face. Elsie taught her hospitality comes before pride, and she had plenty of that to squelch. How dreadful to lose his friendship after growing up with him. Her father sat in an overstuffed chair by the desk and Peter had pulled up a chair beside him. She gazed at the gingerbread while announcing, "These are still warm."

"How thoughtful, my dear." Her father's face beamed. "They smell marvelous."

She longed to interact with Peter as easily. She handed a plate and napkin to her father and then to Peter. For a moment she allowed her gaze to light on his face.

"Thank you." His face was tight.

"Cook will have dinner soon, and you are welcome to stay." Her face grew warm talking to him.

"I should return home and dine there." He paused and swallowed. "My mother—" His eyes watered.

"Of course." Even after all these years, she understood his emotions. "The invitation is open anytime you come."

"Thanks. That means a lot."

"I am sorry about your father."

He nodded.

She couldn't think of more words to say, and left the library.

"Come." Elsie entered the hallway and waved to her. "I be havin' a message for ya."

Mary Beth considered Elsie part of the family since she raised and mothered her from infancy. "From?"

"Your friend, Ida, be handin' a note for ya."

Mary Beth sighed as she read the message Elsie handed her. "Ida says another girl wore a ring Eddie gave her. Or at least that's what she says. How many women did he pursue? I thought he loved me."

"You be a forgetin' that boy. He not bein' worth those tears I see."

Mary Beth rubbed her eyes. "I know."

Elsie drew her close, and Mary Beth snuggled into her ample figure. Eddie had deceived her, so she lost him. Peter wouldn't want her now either.

CHAPTER SIX

Peter's inner pocket bulged with his father's pistol as he rode in the buggy with Mr. Roper. A cool morning breeze wafted across them, and the sun shone in a cloudless sky. Cotton grew in the field to their left, and to the right cornstalks lifted their arms to the sun, each field bordered by a fence. If he had to choose a day to eject a man from his home, even though he'd rather not, he would choose a lovely day like this. "How much further?"

"The Carter farm lies another mile or so from us now." Roper made a clicking sound to the horse. "Mr. Carter will be unhappy, even though he expects us. The homestead was his great- grandfather's."

The thought made Peter cringe. How he would hate to leave property that had been in the family so many years. "What alternatives—"

"None." Roper growled. "This young man has served us lies and deceit now for several years. Your father and I often spoke of *when* this would happen, not *if* it would happen. We have tried being kind, but Carter refuses to do useful labor, and he can't pay his bills."

The reference to his father sobered Peter. His father respected people made in God's image. If Peter could be half the man, he would be grateful. "I understand."

"Look ahead. You can see how the landscape changes." Roper nodded at the property to their right in the distance. Rather than neat rows of crops protected by fences, weeds and underbrush covered the ground. "Carter has allowed the land and house to fall into disrepair. Gambling."

Roper pulled the buggy off the road and tied the horse to a tree. "Let's go."

Peter and Mr. Roper stepped carefully through knee-deep briars avoiding rocks and trash as they headed toward Carter's home. Boards were missing from the steps and porch, and bricks had fallen from the chimney. The white house also needed painting. Paint peeled from the front door, and a nearby window had a large crack in the bottom pane.

"Carter's father owned all eighty acres around the house free and clear. After his death, Henry heavily mortgaged the property," Roper spoke softly. "I have come several times, and the place looks worse each visit."

"Are these steps safe?" Peter pointed to the rotten wood of the stairs.

"They were last month, but I won't risk it." Roper leapt over a couple damaged boards and made it to the porch.

Peter was determined to do even better, so he jumped onto the porch, avoiding the steps altogether.

"Look at that." Roper winked.

A scraping sound caught Peter's attention, and he turned to see a slight man with rounded head and thin blond hair standing at the open door. He threw a metal cup, which crashed at Peter's feet.

"Good morning, Mr. Carter," Roper said. "I am here with my partner, Mr. Chandler."

"Go away." Carter slammed the door.

"You know why we are here?" Roper asked.

"Oh, indeed." He poked his head out of the window beside the door and threw another mug.

Roper dodged it, but he didn't move fast enough. The cup hit him just above the ankle, and he dropped to his knees. "Oww!"

Peter placed a hand on his shoulder. "Do you think anything is broken?"

"Nah." Roper shook his head. "Bruised."

"We are here to foreclose." Peter clenched his fist and faced the door. "Whether you like it or not."

Roper pulled papers from inside his jacket and waved them toward the window. "We have the papers … and guns."

"What now?" Peter looked at Roper.

"We enter. If he resists. We threaten force."

Flexing his muscles, Peter took a deep breath and threw his weight against the front door. It collapsed inward onto the dusty wooden floor. A rancid odor assailed him. A sagging couch with torn upholstery dominated the room. Newspapers and old clothes lay everywhere. Cobwebs hung from the corners. A pile of dirty dishes sat by the kitchen window, and Carter held another cup in his raised hand. "Put that down and come with us. Now."

Carter threw the cup and reached for another.

Peter rolled out of the way and pulled out his gun.

Click. Roper stood in the doorway holding a cocked pistol on Carter. "It's time to go."

The young man shrugged and held up his hands.

"That's better." Roper moved closer. "Do you have a trunk with your things?"

"No." Carter ran a hand through his scraggly blond hair. "I'm not lucky like Chandler's father."

Peter's throat clogged, and he turned his back to hide his emotions. He did not think dying in a train accident made his father lucky.

Roper hobbled into the room and grabbed Carter's arm. "Come. We booked a room for you at the Crutchfield house."

"Luxury." Carter scowled. "I might like that."

"I'll see if I can find clothing." Peter hurried through the house, looking through room after room for a trunk. In the kitchen, he found spoiled food decaying on the rustic table, along with empty bottles of alcohol littering the table and floor. One small room had stacks of leather and animal skins, another had old clothing on top of a rickety bed. Peter picked out a few shirts that appeared the right size and stuffed them into a dirty basket he found on the floor.

He met Roper and Carter at the buggy, for the drive back to Crutchfield House.

Peter hoped they did not have to deal with Carter again.

Frustrating.

Mary Beth's needle came unthreaded. As she reached for more thread on the occasional table beside her, she shut out her friends. Focus. She must get Eddie off her mind. Jane, Ida, and Fanny surrounded her in the Haskell sitting room. All of them were quilting for a girl in their church getting married. (If only she could escape that topic.) The four of them had to complete their section of the quilt today and hand it off to the bride's mother.

Fanny, who sat alone on the red loveseat, put down several pieces of fabric and fiddled with her straight hair. "I can pin them together. But … this pattern …"

"It's hard." Ida occupied a straight chair across the room. She held up several pieces. "Her mother chose it. With all the men going to war and dying, none of us will get married."

Fanny flopped back onto the red love seat. "I hate war."

Mary Beth stopped to blink back tears. She must not lose control. Of course, she'd get sympathy, but she didn't want to face the embarrassment of being jilted.

Jane, who occupied the sofa with Mary Beth, sniffled and pushed a loose lock of hair behind her ear.

Mary Beth sighed. Poor Jane. She must be missing Fred, but she exceled at concealing her feelings. She leaned toward her friend, peering at her work. "Lovely, Jane."

Ida walked over to Jane and gazed at her sewing. "Much better than mine. Did you hear the news? Eddie had another girl in Cleveland. He gave her a charm with a lock of his hair. Did he ever give you anything, Mary Beth?"

Tears clouded Mary Beth's eyes, but she kept her gaze on the fabric in her hands. If Ida kept going, Mary Beth might have to leave before she burst into sobs. She never dreamed Eddie was such a flirt. "His word."

"No." Fannie slapped the love seat, releasing a small cloud of dust. "Does that make five girls?"

Ida mumbled under her breath and counted on her fingers. "Yes. Five. I wonder how many more there were?"

"I need the ... privy." Mary Beth put aside her work and fled. How could she have believed anything Eddie said to her? Would she ever trust a man again? She hated Eddie.

CHAPTER SEVEN

Mary Beth raised her hand to knock on the Chandler's door, then dropped it. "I do not know what to say."

Jane rolled her eyes. "You came to return the scissors."

"I know." Mary Beth took a deep breath. "But I didn't visit at all after …"

"Mary Beth, this isn't like you."

Death. Who wanted to confront that? She gazed at the impressive roses engraved in the woodwork. "I should have come by and offered condolences. I don't even recall this fancy trim around the front door."

"Is it because of Peter?" Jane narrowed her eyes.

"No. It's just that Mrs. Chandler always seemed so perfect, in control. But that didn't answer your question. Yes, he is home now."

"He will be at work. Here. Mention these." Jane held up the package from her mother.

"I guess … comforting someone older. How does one do that?"

"You can." Jane placed a hand on her arm. "That Sunday after we heard about Fred, you saw what I tried to hide."

An image from Mary Beth's childhood flash into her mind. Mrs. Chandler stood over her and frowned when she and Peter had been too loud. Right now, Mary Beth felt as small as she did that day. "But—"

The door flew open and Ruth stood slumping, her

brown hair was mussed, and she bore a big frown. "Hi."

Her droopy mannerisms worried Mary Beth, and she scooped the girl into her arms. Loving Ruth was easy. "You seem disturbed. How can I help?"

Ruth snuggled closer, sniffling. "I ... miss you."

Mary Beth recalled the many hours they had walked through the woods and chatted. "Me too. We came to return your mom's scissors. But you look unhappy."

"Mama ... she's been crying."

"Oh." Mary Beth's stomach dropped, and she glanced toward Jane for support.

Jane caressed Ruth's youthful face. "May we come in?"

Ruth nodded and broke free from Mary Beth's hug. "Come with me."

Mary Beth and Jane followed her to the sitting room. Alarmed, Mary Beth ran to the light blue sofa where Peter's mother lay curled sobbing into the fabric. Tears stung Mary Beth's eyes just watching the older lady. She knelt beside Mrs. Chandler, taking her hand. "Let's send for Peter."

Jane placed a hand on Mrs. Chandler's forehead. "I agree. We also need a damp cloth—for her face."

Ruth rang the bell and ran to the door. "Ask Billy for the cloth. I shall fetch my brother."

The girl's sudden burst of energy pleased Mary Beth. Ruth probably needed something to do. "Your Mama will be fine. Jane and I will stay with her."

Jane nodded. "Be off with you."

Ruth dashed from the room.

Mary Beth looked around. Here she sat holding Mrs. Chandler's hand, which seemed unreal. She never dreamed Peter's mother would need consolation. Peter would arrive, and she had dumped him for Eddie. Could she look him in the eye? If only she had avoided Eddie, she wouldn't be in this mess.

C&R BANK

Tense all over, Peter sat in Mr. Roper's office on the other side of his huge desk, writing as fast as he could. The ticking of the grandfather clock behind him reminded Peter the sooner he memorized bank policies, the sooner he could immerse himself in work. Mr. Roper had carried on alone for months now, and Peter must do his share. He paused to dip his quill in Roper's ornate inkwell. "Let me see … I hope I recall all this … should I—"

Roper sat back in his leather chair and chuckled. "Slow down. Your father planned to guide you for a year."

Peter stopped. A memory flashed into his mind of his father in that same chair, but Peter suppressed the thought. He was here to work. "When I graduated, I thought I knew everything, but all this is overwhelming. I must step in to help you."

"In time, you can." Roper pursed his lips. "I'd rather you take on responsibility slowly—as you feel secure. Remember to care about the customer, regardless of who they might be. If we become friends, we keep their business."

"Once we confirm their good character."

"Of course … for us and them. Banking requires absolute integrity. Once that goes, your bank is dying."

Mr. Riddle, the bank secretary, knocked lightly on the

door before stepping in. Peter had never seen him without a pencil behind his ear and a pad of paper in his hands. He grimaced. "I hate to disturb …"

"You never disturb me, Riddle." Roper shrugged and stuck his reading glasses in his coat pocket. "Mr. Chandler could use a break."

"Uh, yes, sir." Riddle cleared his throat. "I wasn't quite sure what to do. A man is here from Crutchfield House … regarding Mr. Carter."

"What?" Peter spun around to face Riddle. He had worried Carter would be difficult.

"It seems he has demanded more than we paid for." Riddle gestured toward the door. "They sent a porter who would like to talk to you."

"Ah. I see." Roper massaged his forehead. "Send this man in."

"I look forward to seeing how you handle this." Peter folded his arms. Roper had been very generous to give Carter a place to stay and food. The law didn't require that. "Isn't Crutchfield House a client?"

"Yes." Roper inhaled. "As for handling this … I am praying."

Both men shared a laugh, but they stopped when they heard Riddle outside the door.

"This way, please." Riddle opened the door, and a man wearing a dark blue porter's uniform walked in.

Roper stood and extended his hand. "How can I help you, Mr.—"

Peter followed his partner's lead and offered his hand also. "I am Mr. Gray. The manager sent me because Mr. Carter has demanded food and drink beyond what you paid for. We wondered if you wanted to add money or whether should we refuse him service."

Roper cringed. "I apologize. I did not anticipate this."

"You can understand," the porter continued. "We do not want to offend."

"Such kindness." Roper offered a pleasant smile. "I appreciate all your efforts, but … there's no need to provide anything further. He's a gambler."

"I understand, sir." The porter bowed and backed toward the door. "Thank you."

"Please come whenever you have questions," Roper said. "Anytime." Peter let out his breath when the door closed behind the porter. "Carter is quite a character."

"Indeed. One must value true gold rather than that which glitters. You can see the outcome." Roper tapped the desk. "I will gift the hotel after Carter leaves. Any thoughts on what they would like?"

What a clever idea. Peter ran his hand over his face in thought.

Breath lost and hair disheveled, Ruth rushed into the room. "Petie, it's Mother. She can't stop crying."

Peter could barely catch his breath after running all the way home. The sitting room resembled a hospital. Jane stood by a table covered in a white cloth that held a basin of water. His mother, draped in a blanket, reclined on the sofa in Mary Beth's arms. Jane blotted his mother's face and hands with a damp towel. Strands of Mama's hair hung about her face and several stuck to her dampened cheeks. Her eyes were red, and her clothing was rumpled. He worried his absence at such a crucial time had made her distraught. As a new widow, she had no one to support her, and he regretted taking so long to return. Unsure what to do or say, he watched helplessly as Mary Beth crooned over his mother. How embarrassing. "Mama?"

She glanced at him and crumpled in another outburst of weeping. "Why didn't you come home last night? I assumed …"

He pulled an overstuffed chair close and took Mother's hand. The sight of her made him unable to recall what he'd done the day before.

Jane spoke up, "Ruth was terribly upset about losing her father. Your mother has been very strong for her. I checked in often, and I believe this is the first time she's given way to her feelings."

"I appreciate your kindness." He meant both Mary Beth and Jane, but he avoided their eyes.

Peter looked over his mother's head toward the photo of his father above the fireplace. How he wished he could ask for advice. Would he be able to work, or must he stay home?

Oh God! I must have guidance.

CHAPTER EIGHT

Morning fog cloaked the city as Peter headed toward the bank. He glanced at his watch and picked up his pace, so he could arrive before opening time. Several issues came to mind he wanted to speak with Roper about before work overwhelmed them. Sweat trickled down his brow, and he pulled out his handkerchief. People hurried by him. As he neared the bank, he saw a crowd gathered at the front door. Every banker feared a run on the bank because it could destroy the business. Peter broke into a run. As he neared the area, he noticed the cluster of people pushing each other. "Move away from the door."

"Leave me alone!"

"I need my money," a man shouted.

"The city must not leave the Confederacy."

Indistinct shouting.

"I want my money, so I can get out of the Confederacy," someone screamed.

"The Confederacy is not evil," another hollered.

"Secede from the Confederacy!"

"Get your hands off me."

"Secede. Go back to the Union."

"Stop shoving."

"I must get to the teller first."

"Rejoin the Union."

Peter elbowed his way to the front door. If the crowd didn't disperse, someone could be trampled. Raising his voice, he shouted, "We do *not* serve unruly crowds. Please leave."

A man shouted, "No. We came for our money, and we will stay until we get it."

Three men started yelling at each other, and fists flew.

Peter lunged toward the three and pulled them apart until one slammed him in the stomach. He crumpled forward, trying to breathe, but managed to stay on his feet. "Leave quietly. Now." he said. His voice weak, he hoped he spoke with authority.

Roper came from the back of the building, brandishing a rifle. "I shall use this if anyone becomes violent. Go home now. We will not open today."

The yelling died down.

"Go home." Roper bellowed again. "Now."

The crowd thinned, but a few men shoved others as they walked away.

Dizzy and nauseated, his heart pounding, Peter sank onto the wooden sidewalk by the door.

Roper assisted several people to their feet, then he knelt in the dirt beside another man who lay on his face. "Sir … sir? Peter, he's … dead."

Oh no. Peter had worried someone would get hurt. He rose to help, but staggered and sat back down.

"Are you all right, Peter?" Mr. Roper asked.

"I need a moment."

"I shall send for the doctor." Roper turned the body over. "It's Edward Harden."

C&R Bank Foyer

Peter sat at the front desk looking up into the face of Dr. Milo Smith, a thin man with salt and pepper hair and a goatee. How comforting to see the doctor who had cared for him all his life. The beloved man had a calming influence on his patients, and many baby boys in the city bore his name. "I am fine."

Smith raised his brows while taking Peter's pulse. "Uh-huh. Tell me what happened."

Peter gave a description. "Harden needs you worse than I do."

"Not a chance. Your heart rate is rapid, and your face is pale. I want you home in bed, and I shall visit you again in a couple of hours. Mind now. I can give quite a scold."

Peter thought it best to change the subject. "I suppose the crowd trampled Mr. Harden?"

"No." The doctor closed his black bag. "Broken neck. He was dead before he hit the ground."

Peter's jaw dropped. "The crowd was restless but ... that sounds like murder."

Dr. Smith shrugged. "Emotions out of control—"

"I left Mr. Riddle guarding the door, Peter." Roper had just entered from outside and turned to the doctor. "Your assistants are removing the body now. What do you need?"

"*You* need to rest." The doctor put a hand on Mr. Roper's shoulder. "You have been doing the job of two men ever since Chandler died. Did the sheriff come?"

"He is here along with several Confederate soldiers," Roper said.

"Humpf. We do *not* need them."

"Papa. What is going on?" Mary Beth walked up to her father and kissed his cheek. She wore blue and looked particularly fetching. "Peter? What? You are ... injured?"

Peter cringed at the tone of her voice. He did not want her hovering over him like his mother would do.

"Indeed," Dr. Smith said. "I am about to suggest both Peter and your father keep the bank closed at least today and tomorrow. Our citizens are explosive, and both of you should be resting."

Mary Beth's face softened. "What happened?"

Roper chuckled. "A few angry citizens, that's all dear."

"That sounds dreadful," Mary Beth frowned. "And what of Peter?"

"I am fine," Peter protested. When he went home, he would receive the full-blown-mama mode, and he didn't want more.

"Peter heroically separated a fracas," Roper said. "But he is tough."

Mary Beth rushed to his side and touched his shoulder. "I am so sorry."

Peter squirmed. At least she was talking to him, though.

ROPER HOME

Mary Beth tiptoed up to her father's bedroom and peeked in. Her father lay on his side, snoring. Good. He had been working too hard for too long. If only she had pulled back the ornate bedspread that once belonged to her mother. Any damage to the fabric would upset her, but she must remember she valued her father far more than a mere bedspread she could replace. At least, she had remembered to pull the heavy drapes so the room would be dark, and he could sleep longer.

Making as little noise as possible, she headed downstairs to think and plan. Once she wormed a description of the mob from her father, she was horrified. Obviously, her fellow citizens held contradictory views, and many were angry. Her mind refused to believe her father had threatened the crowd with a gun. If one of those men had come with his own gun, they might have seen bloodshed. Her heart trembled at the thought of losing her father or Peter.

Alert and wary, she would snatch her father's newspapers and attempt to overhear his conversations, so she could be aware of danger. Someone killed a man, and if she could find the culprit, everyone would be safer. Maybe she should make herself some notes on how to proceed. If only her relationship with Peter wasn't so strained, he would have ideas.

Perhaps renewing their friendship would be a good place to start.

Surrounded by two walls filled with leather-bound volumes, Peter sat back in the huge leather chair in his father's library. This was the most comfortable he'd been all day. His stomach was sore, but at this angle, he felt no pain. He inhaled the familiar smell of books, and he felt close to his father amongst his notes, records, and household accounts. Mother had felt stronger today, and she had visited the butcher and grocer. In her absence, he had time to sort his thoughts.

What could he do to avoid the scene he'd witnessed today? He could arrive before the bank opened, which he had intended to do this morning. Perhaps he could also carry a loaded gun at all times. Roper's weapon had dispersed the crowd right away, but how dreadful Mr. Harden lost his life. Peter could also pray for calm to return to the city.

He must not forget to reach out to Harden's wife. C&R Bank looked for ways to help widows, not only while they grieved but on a regular basis.

Footsteps down the hall alarmed him. Surely Mama had not returned quite so soon.

"Peter?" His mother opened the door. "There you are. I met Dr. Smith in town, and he told me you should be in bed."

"I am quite comfortable here." He wouldn't tell mother about the documents in his briefcase. When everyone had gone to bed, he planned to read and catch up on work. Reading could not be strenuous.

"No." She burst into tears. "I cannot ... lose you."

Peter sighed. His mother didn't need more distress. Nor did he want to be smothered by her mothering.

CHAPTER NINE

Despite lingering soreness, Peter woke hungry with the mingled aroma of sausage and biscuits. He rose and moved about the room, dressing in his robe to see how he felt. He crept downstairs and turned right into the dining room. His mother sat at the table with her back to him, bowls of eggs and other breakfast foods in front of her. Still quite sore, he stood as straight as he could as he walked in so his mother would not fuss over him. If he stayed home another day, he would not retain his sanity. The moment he finished breakfast, he would send a message to Roper to see if the bank would open. He needed to be productive.

"Oh." His mother jumped. "Sorry. I thought you were Andrew."

He leaned down to hug her and headed to his usual chair.

"Peter." His mother grabbed his arm. "Please take the seat at the head of the table."

"But that's where—"

"I know. But I would feel better if you sat there. It feels so … empty."

He hesitated, then glancing at her face he slid into the chair. She appeared pleased, and he relaxed.

He sat down and ate a biscuit and sausage, savoring the home cooked food. Yawning and running her fingers through her dark hair, Ruth stumbled in the room. Squealing, her eyes grew wide. "That's Daddy's chair,

Petie."

Peter froze.

"Ruthie, dear, I requested he sit there. I feel much safer, not that I do not miss your daddy."

Tears exploded from Ruth, and she darted out.

Peter shot up, toppling the chair over, his face hot. Squelching tears, he shifted his mind to the bank. "I had best contact Mr. Roper—"

"I shall speak with Ruth. She handles her grief differently." His mother rose and touched his face. "Mr. Roper sent a note for you to come to his house. I think he intends to keep the bank closed today. There's no rush. Have some tea, so we can talk for a moment."

"Mama, I cannot replace Dad." Already the responsibility weighed on him.

"Of course not. However, your presence is soothing."

"I shall see you tonight." Peter walked around her to dress for the day.

"But, darling, you must eat breakfast." His mother tapped his shoulder.

"I have eaten enough." He kissed her cheek. She was acting as if she was his mother now, and a few moments ago, she was looking to him as a provider. He shook his head. This new role challenged him, and he had not even done much banking yet.

Mary Beth kept her ears attuned to the front door while she updated accounts receivable in her father's library. She adored working alongside her father while sitting in a smaller chair next to his father huge black one. However, this morning, her father had asked Peter to join them. She wondered if his presence would change the comradery. Perhaps she could act as if Eddie had never entered their lives and see how Peter responded.

Her dad shifted in his chair and winced.

"Papa? Is something amiss?"

"My shoulder is sore from lifting." He winked at her. "My girl worries too much."

She tensed as the housekeeper's voice echoed down the hallway.

"Mr. Chandler, you be knowin' me. There be no reason for you to a knockin' on that door. Jus' come right on in, sir. I be feelin' like yous one of my own, son."

"Maud, you know me too." Peter's voice was softer. "And I knock."

The housekeeper's laughter grew louder as she opened the door. "Mr. Peter be here."

"Welcome, Peter." Dad stood and held out his hand. "We have some important things to discuss."

Mary Beth scrambled to pull up a chair for her old friend.

Peter took it from her. "I can do that. But thanks."

She felt herself get warm, but she was being polite.

"I want your opinion, Peter. Did you think Harden's sudden death interesting?" Mary Beth's father tapped his finger on his desk.

Peter rubbed his chin as he sat. "Not initially, no. However, I don't know these people as you do. But I can see where you might be concerned."

"What?" Mary Beth tugged on her father's sleeve. "Tell me what happened."

"Mary Beth, Harden had concerns about Carter. The

timing bothered me. If anyone else had been killed, I would have no suspicion."

"Did you have any reason to doubt Harden?" Peter asked.

"No. I have never known him to be untruthful, and living so close to Carter, he would learn things others might not know," her father said. "I never made our plans to foreclose public."

Mary Beth crossed her arms. "Did either of you see Mr. Carter there?"

"I didn't." Peter shrugged. "We have heard nothing further about him."

Her father shook his head. "I didn't see him either."

Mary Beth snatched a fresh piece of paper. "I shall ask our employees who they saw. If I find someone we know and trust, it's possible they will remember who came that day also."

"Dearest, you may ask those we employ, but leave customers to us. If someone did intend to murder, that person would have no qualms about doing it again."

"But, Papa, no one suspects murder, so I should be able to ask questions." Mary Beth twisted a lock of hair. "Everyone assumes Mr. Harden fell and the crowd trampled him."

"The murderer will not be deceived." Peter gazed right into her eyes. "According to Dr. Smith, it's unlikely this was an accident."

"Yes. I hadn't thought of that. I shall take care. All we need is an excuse, like finding a button. I can say we must find the owner and that means we must know who was there."

"Dearest, politics has made our city angry and

unfriendly." Her father patted her hand. "That's not a great atmosphere for a lady. Mr. Strong has announced he's leaving to join the military. You can fill in for him and leave this to us."

"Can we carry out banking without politics?" Peter said.

"I am not so sure," Mary Beth said. "My friend's father was pretty upset yesterday when I visited. He said he would not use a bank that does not agree with his views."

"That's why I keep my own views private. However, the sharp divisions make us more likely to have a riot or worse." Her father sighed.

Papa appeared so tired. She would assist him, so he could rest more. Asking a few questions never hurt anyone.

Later that Afternoon
C&R Bank Office

"Well, Papa, this is odd." Mary Beth glared at the ledger in her hand. Perhaps she was looking at the wrong date. She had accompanied her father to the post office and then to the bank. Now she sat in a chair opposite her father's mahogany desk, looking over the ledger entries the day Harden died. Papa occupied the executive chair on the other side of the desk, sorting through a stack of files with his back to her.

Her father swiveled around. "Odd?"

"Yes." Mary Beth rubbed her forehead. "My eyes must be getting tired."

He winked at her. "Let me see. My eyes are sharpest in the early afternoon."

She crossed the plush carpet as she took the ledger and teller receipts to her father. "See, the day before the mob, Mrs. Harden came to withdraw $1.50, and then later that afternoon she deposited $1.50. Did that happen the same day?"

His brows drew together. "I believe you are correct. I suspect she has a very ordinary story to explain her actions."

"I would like to know what Mr. Harden planned to do at the bank too." Mary Beth sat back in her chair, allowing ideas to flood her mind. "I wonder if they had a disagreement over money, and he was going to withdraw the money again? Or maybe she thought she had to pay a bill, and her husband already paid it?"

"I doubt unearthing that mystery will assist us." Papa offered her a playful grin.

"I should take her some of Cook's pastries and offer my sympathy. That's appropriate and kind."

"You have not paid your respects?" Her father pulled a mock frown. "You have blackened our name by failing your civic duties."

"Papa, your secretary always sends condolences, and it happened so recently. We are well within the reasonable time for calling."

"Call on her." Her father's bushy eyebrows rose. "But confine your conversation to sympathy."

"Yes, sir."

CHAPTER TEN

THE NEXT MORNING

Peter entered the bank foyer, prepared to greet customers on his way out, but he found the room empty except for Mr. Grant at the teller window, and Mr. Riddle at the front desk. Peter pulled a list from his inner pocket. If only he could envision the first client he was heading out to visit. Surely his father had introduced them a couple years ago, and this man—the printer—might not be pleased with Peter's poor memory.

The bell tinkled as the bank door opened.

Peter snapped to attention and extended his hand to the chubby man dressed in a beige jacket and dark pants. "I am Peter Chandler. May I help you, sir?"

"Hello." The man doffed his hat, revealing unruly auburn hair. "My name is George Owen. I am Mr. Carter's cousin and heir. In light of his death, I am here to take up mortgage payments."

How unexpected. "My partner and I saw Mr. Carter less than a week ago to serve eviction papers. At the time, he was fine."

"Indeed." He whipped a large white handkerchief out of his pocket and blotted his face. "He was my last relative. He came to visit after the foreclosure. I found him this morning at the bottom of the basement stairs. Dead."

Peter would need guidance with this situation, and he hated not knowing what to do. "If you will take a seat, just past that desk, let me speak to my partner."

"Of course." Owen swiped his face again and put away his handkerchief while sniffling.

Peter darted upstairs into Mr. Roper's office. "Sir?"

Mr. Roper's eyebrows went up. "I did not expect you back so soon."

"I never left." Peter nodded toward the foyer. "We have a Mr. Owen downstairs who claims to be Carter's cousin. He said Carter is dead, and he wants to take on the mortgage and occupy the property. I was not sure of bank policies."

Roper closed the ledger he worked on. "Pull Carter's file and bring this man upstairs."

A few moments later, Peter seated Mr. Owen in front of Mr. Roper's desk.

Peter seated himself beside Roper, behind the desk. "I am sorry to hear the news of Mr. Carter's death. When did this happen?"

"He came to me after ... being ejected." Owen coughed. "Soon afterward, he fell ill and died."

"And this was ..." Mr. Roper tapped his fingers on the desk.

"He arrived day before yesterday." Owen held up his chin and looked down on them. "This morning, I found him dead."

Roper nodded. "I will need a death certificate."

"I don't have it—yet," Owen said.

"You are aware Carter made no payments for the last nine months?" Roper said.

"Yes." Owen leaned forward. "I am prepared to offer

you a large Confederate bond as earnest. Upon maturity, it will be worth much more than the money my cousin owed."

"You have that now?" Peter asked. He hadn't even seen one yet.

"No. But I shall obtain one," Owen said.

"We will accept gold." Mr. Roper opened the file. "You must pay all the back rent, and we charge a five-dollar fee for paperwork involved in taking over the payments."

Owen turned red. "You refuse a Confederate bond?"

"Yes, sir." Roper crossed his arms. "However, you didn't even bring one."

"Unbelievable!" He stood and stomped to the door. "You shall hear from my lawyer."

As Owen thundered down the stairs, Peter turned to Roper. "Does this create a problem for us?"

"He can file a complaint in court and spread anger around town." Roper rose to leave. "In light of the present mood of Chattanooga residents, we could lose citizens loyal to the Confederacy."

Peter rubbed the back of his neck. "I have heard Union sympathizers are leaving."

"True." Roper paused at his office door. "The war Lincoln started might change their allegiance, because no one wants to be invaded."

"So, this could ruin our business?" Peter frowned.

"Indeed." Mr. Roper cleared his throat. "However, I am not about to accept paper that has no value. As bankers, we must value gold, just as a Christian must value God's truth."

"Very sound." Peter understood, but he had hoped for less upheaval in his first few months at the bank. At this point, he had too much to learn about everyday banking to weather a crisis.

THAT EVENING
ROPER LIBRARY

Mary Beth yawned while turning a page in her book. Darkness had fallen, and she kept thinking about going to bed. However, she enjoyed reading in the library, which had two oil lamps. One spread light across her reading, the other sat on her father's desk where he worked.

Crash!

She looked up and tossed aside the book. Her father had fallen onto the desk where he'd been working, toppling the oil lamp beside him. The oil dripping onto the Oriental rug burst into flames, catching a few papers that had fallen off the desk. The fire blazed up fast and moved toward the bookcase behind him. "Papa? Papa!"

When he did not respond she screamed and threw her shawl over the fire while stomping on the blaze. "Fire! Fire!"

Maud ran in with a pitcher of tea and tossed its contents over the fire before it reached the books. "Lands sake, child. Ya be a burnin' those pretty feet."

Mary Beth stomped out the remaining sparks as she wheezed and coughed. Black smoke filled the room. "I am unhurt, Maud. But Papa is ill."

Elsie ran in. "Oh, lordy, lordy. Your pa. I best be a fetchin' doctor. You get outside an breathe, girl."

Heaving with each breath, she obeyed, rushing into the cool evening air. Rather than collapse on the porch she inched toward the Haskell's home, stopping to rest every few feet.

She proceeded as fast as she could the entire half-mile while still coughing. No lights illumined the darkened house, but she pounded on the front door anyway.

The butler answered, "Yes, ma'am?"

"Help! Fire!" She pointed toward her house. The image of her father slumped over his desk had seared into her mind. If something happened to him, she would die. "Send for the doctor ... my father."

Wearing a housecoat, Jane peeked around the butler, her mother and father appearing with her. Jane gasped and rushed toward her.

"Is the fire still burning?" Mrs. Haskell asked, glancing toward Mary Beth's home.

"No." Inhaling hurt. She slid onto the porch, exhausted.

Coughing and wheezing, Mary Beth pulled away as Jane tried to help her. "Soot ..."

"Get Milo Smith right away," ordered Mr. Haskell as he swept Mary Beth up in his arms and carried her inside.

"No." Mary Beth shook her head, wishing she had stayed home. "I should see to Father."

Mr. Haskell carried her up to Jane's bedroom and deposited her on the bed. "You are injured."

Mary Beth squirmed, hoping to get away as Mr. Haskell placed her on the bed. "Have someone check on my father. He must be very ill not to respond to the fire."

Jane brushed Mary Beth's hair back from her forehead. "You must not jeopardize your own health."

The maid arrived with a bowl of water, and Jane sponged off her face. "I do not think you realize your own injuries, Mary Beth. Even your eyes are bloodshot. We shall see to your father."

"Ouch!" The water stung her face. She coughed up black mucus tinged with blood, and shivered at the sight. How much smoke got in her lungs?

Jane helped her bathe and change into a soft nightgown. Time crawled. All she could think of was her papa.

Dr. Smith entered the room with his black bag and asked what happened.

Mary Beth gave the details while the doctor's gaze roamed her face. "I am worried about Father. Please see him first."

"I have your father well in hand, but you have burns around your nose." He pulled out a tongue depressor. "Open your mouth."

She obeyed until coughing overtook her again.

"You have burns inside your throat as well. If the tissue swells, you might find breathing difficult, so you must stay in bed for several days."

Mary Beth blinked and rubbed her eyes. How could she solve their problems from bed?

"Keep your hands away from your eyes too." He turned to Jane. "I shall prescribe medication, including drops for her eyes. If her breathing becomes labored, prop her up on pillows."

"I cannot be very sick," Mary Beth said. "We had the fire under control in a few minutes."

"Your sense of time could be distorted." He placed several bottles of medicine on the table by the bed. "Rest. I shall be caring for your father."

Jane handed her a cup filled with medicine, and Mary Beth recoiled at the bitterness. Her head and chest hurt.

She must see Mrs. Harden soon. As her body grew limp, she worried when the doctor would allow her out of bed.

CHAPTER ELEVEN

THE NEXT MORNING

Light rain brought a pleasant coolness. Peter removed his hat to shake off the water as he entered the bank. Several customers already stood at the teller window in the foyer. Peter nodded at a few as he headed up the stairs to the office.

Mr. Riddle, the bank secretary, stepped forward as Peter reached the landing at the top of the steps. He held up a slip of paper. "Mr. Chandler, a gentleman came to see Mr. Roper. However, your partner has not arrived. I thought you might agree to meet with him—Mr. James—since he has been waiting."

The bank had changed so much that Peter wouldn't have the answers. If he could delay a few minutes, Roper would arrive. Besides, he'd just arrived. "Give me ten minutes."

Riddle nodded.

Peter didn't hurry as he removed his raincoat and shifted several files from the desk, but his partner didn't arrive. He rang for Mr. Riddle to bring the visitor.

Mr. Riddle escorted a man in a gray suit with black hair to the door. "Mr. Chandler, this is Mr. James. He is a lawyer from Nashville."

"You have come a long way to see me." Peter stood and

offered his hand. "How may I assist you, sir?"

Mr. James walked toward him with a pronounced limp. "I am here on behalf of George Owen, cousin of the late Mr. Carter."

Peter's stomach knotted. "Please continue."

"Mr. Owen has a legitimate claim to the property, and he became livid when he heard you are trying to sell his land."

"We are willing for Mr. Owen to take up the mortgage if he will pay the amount owed. However, that opportunity ends when the month ends. So, he must be hasty."

Mr. James shook his head. "My client instructed me to file suit in court if you do not comply with his wishes."

Peter held in a groan. The bank could not afford hefty legal fees. "We must have a death certificate to proceed, and Mr. Owen couldn't provide one."

"He said you had the document already."

"We do not," Peter said. "However, I would like to consult with my partner, who should be here any time."

"In that case, I shall drop by later today."

Peter walked Mr. James to the door. "Mr. Riddle, could you see Mr. James out?"

"Of course, sir." Riddle rose. "Dr. Smith is waiting downstairs. Should I send him up?"

"Please."

"Good morning, sir." Peter shook the doctor's hand.

"Indeed. I am thankful for the rain. My herbs were far too dry." Smith put down his black bag.

"Forgive me, sir. You appear tense. How may I help you?"

"I wish I didn't have sad news." Dr. Smith rubbed his goatee. "Mr. Roper had a severe heart attack last night.

He fell onto the desk in his library and started a small fire. Mary Beth has some burns in her nose and throat. I fear both will indisposed for a while."

Peter sank into his chair, nauseated. He might not have guidance with the lawyer after all. Even worse he might be running the bank alone, which meant he could make serious mistakes. On top of all that, he still cared for Mary Beth a great deal. He found himself longing for the days when the two played together as friends. "How serious is Roper?"

"Very dangerous." The doctor crossed his arms. "I worried he might not live through the night."

"Does Mary Beth know his condition?"

Dr. Smith shook her head. "She inhaled smoke. While her injuries are not life threatening, they can create serious problems if not treated carefully. She is on bedrest at the Haskell's home. I do not want her to know the full extent of her father's injuries yet."

God help me!

THE HASKELL HOME

As the sun rose, Mary Beth woke, sat up, and swallowed. She felt fine except for a slight soreness in her throat. The clock by the bed showed the time to be eight in the morning, much later than her father got up. She had slept in Jane's bed under a lovely coverlet, while Jane had slept upright in a wing chair beside her. Surely the events of last night weren't tragic enough to make her friend endure that. Besides Mary Beth promised her father she'd visit

Mrs. Harden today. She must carry out her responsibilities. She slid her feet to the floor and stood. The room spun for a moment, but several deep breaths steadied her.

"What are you doing?" Wide-eyed, Jane stared at her.

"I promised—I would see Mrs. Harden."

"The doctor said you must rest, and Mama wanted us to sleep all morning after our late night. I'm sure she's in bed." Jane shook her head. "What's the emergency anyway?"

"I feel fine. I can go alone, so you won't have to dress. There's a discrepancy with Mrs. Harden's bank account I must clear up for father."

"Ha. I think not." Jane put her hands on her hips. "I am coming with you. Mama would be furious if I didn't. Besides, what time is it?"

"A few minutes past eight." Mary Beth reached for her gown laying across a chest at the foot of the bed. "Mrs. Harden lives five miles from here. She will be up when we arrive."

"You cannot wear that. It reeks of smoke." Jane ran to her armoire and pulled out two dresses. "Here. Take this one, and I shall notify the groom. Perhaps we can slip out without rousing Mama."

Jane dressed and combed her hair.

Mary Beth did the same, dressing faster than she ever had. "Let's leave together out the back. The house seems quiet."

"Papa is up, but he won't hear anything." Jane fixed a couple buttons Mary Beth couldn't reach. "I hope I do not regret this."

Tiptoeing, Mary Beth followed her friend down several hallways and staircases to a door that led to the stable. Once outside, she whispered, "I don't recall going this way."

Jane whispered back, "I used the servant's entrance. It's closer to the stables. Hang back. Let me talk to the groom. I want him to keep this quiet." She disappeared.

A young man driving a buggy came around from the back side of the stables a few minutes later.

"I found a gift. Mother leaves these for the grooms, and it has fresh cookies." Jane walked out the door she had entered, holding a tin of cookies in her arms. "Let's go before my mother wakes."

"Good." Mary Beth had forgotten about taking food. She looked up at the house as someone, maybe Mrs. Chandler, pulled back the drapes. She ran to the buggy.

LAWYER'S OFFICE

Peter's gaze fell on the huge bookcases that dominated his lawyer's office, covering three walls. Those books served as proof this man knew more than he did. Even though Peter had a degree from a prestigious school, he would require the same guidance a child might need as he learned how to ride a racehorse. He had just graduated from a wooden rocking horse in banking experience. His actions could sink the bank.

Mr. Gray, a tall, lanky man with dark hair, and thin face, entered and shut the door. "Please be seated, Mr. Chandler."

Peter almost looked around for his father, and then realized the lawyer spoke to him. He eased into the chair in front of the desk that dwarfed the one he used in the bank office. "I have just returned from a European trip, and my partner has suffered a severe heart attack. How much can I do in his absence?"

"In terms of your father's will, you own fifty-one percent of the bank, which means you may carry on banking duties the same way your father did."

"Up until this point, Mr. Roper has made all the decisions. What about agreements my partner made before I arrived?"

Gray tucked his chin. "You cannot override any agreement he signed unless you have power of attorney."

Peter shifted in his chair as he considered the vastness of the job he must do alone. "Roper is so ill, the doctor fears for his life."

Gray gazed upward while caressing his chin. "I understand his daughter is his heir. She might have paperwork that allows her the right to sign for him."

"Mary Beth might still be unaware of her father's condition. She was injured the night he became ill, so I am hesitant to approach her right now."

"I see. With your permission, I can speak with his attorney—"

"He uses Mr. Haskell."

"Yes, I can approach him. Roper may have provided for this."

Peter must avoid a hefty legal bill, yet, he would have little time since he'd be doing his job and Mr. Roper's. He turned the two problems over in his mind. "I shall visit Mr. Haskell myself. Thanks for the offer."

He valued his relationship with God more than ever now. Without divine guidance, Peter would fail.

CHAPTER TWELVE

Once out in the buggy, Mary Beth found her throat more irritated than she expected, and she tried not to cough. Jane would scold her for insisting they go, but Mary Beth hoped to discover Mrs. Harden's motive for her strange behavior. She kept Jane chattering by asking questions or commenting on the lush landscape. At last, they arrived. The gray house had a small porch with ornate railings. Red shutters completed the look. "Jane, isn't the house lovely?"

Jane giggled. "Yes. It's almost as pretty as mine."

Mary Beth and Jane walked up porch steps that looked recently painted, and Mary Beth knocked on the door.

A slender maid wearing a white apron and matching scarf answered. "May I help you?"

Mary Beth offered her gift. "I am from C&R bank, and I wanted to express my sympathy for the death of Mr. Harden. We brought a gift."

"How very kind." She opened the door and took the tin. "Mrs. Harden will be pleased."

"Is she available?" Mary Beth tried to see around the maid into the hallway. Several large plants stood in the narrow windows beside the door. A strong odor assailed her, and she began coughing.

"Please come in." The servant opened the door wider. "I shall ask. Mrs. Harden has been unwell for several days."

Once inside the foyer, the cloying odor made it hard

for Mary Beth to breathe, and her coughing grew worse. Rather than follow the lady down the hall, she stood near the door, tearing up.

"Should we ask the maid for water?" Jane patted her on the back.

Mary Beth shook her head, still coughing. How embarrassing to visit someone and be unable to talk.

The maid left for a few minutes, and Mary Beth opened the front door for a second to allow in fresh air.

Jane rubbed her back. "I think we'd best leave."

"But … I promised …" The very thought made Mary Beth want to scream. How maddening to be so close and unable to complete the chore.

The maid returned and curtsied. "Mrs. Harden is too ill for a visit, but she begged you to return. Her daughter comes home in a week or so, and she wants you to meet her."

Unable to talk, Mary Beth kept choking back a cough.

"Then we will call again." Jane said, putting a hand on Mary Beth's arm. "We would love to meet her."

"Yes. I think she would be pleased." The maid nodded.

"What is her name?" Jane asked.

"Miss Beverly Harden."

"Goodbye." Jane held the front door open for Mary Beth. Once they climbed into the carriage, she said, "I would have been coughing too if we'd stayed. The odor was horrid."

Mary Beth breathed easier in the fresh air, but she was upset with herself. She sensed she would get answers from Mrs. Harden. At least Jane hadn't said she should have stayed in bed.

CRUTCHFIELD HOUSE

After consulting with his lawyer, Peter dropped by the Crutchfield House to see the manager. He wanted to ensure the hotel staff received the pastries he'd sent from the bank, and to make sure the food was the highest quality. As he hurried across the plush carpet to the marbled counter, he saw Mr. Weston coming toward him. Peter had always admired the wealthy man's suave and gentlemanly manners. He emanated confidence. Today he wore the usual navy suit perfectly pressed and had every dark hair in place, even the small streak of gray in the front.

"What a pleasure to see you here." Mr. Weston extended his hand to Peter.

Peter shook his hand, wondering if the financier had purchased the hotel. Roper reported citizens turned to Weston for loans if the bank hesitated. "And you, of course. I haven't seen you since I came home."

"I do apologize." Weston put a hand on Peter's shoulder. "I should have called with condolences, but since your father passed away several months back, the obligation slipped my mind. How sad for your entire family. I hope your dear mother and sister are well?"

"Indeed." Normally Peter didn't mind a congenial chat, but the mention of his father almost brought tears.

"I understand you have foreclosed on the Carter property." Weston pulled his eyebrows together, seemingly concerned. "I would be delighted to purchase the land right away."

Peter swallowed as Weston named a large sum, which

would benefit the bank. "We must clear up a legal issue before we sell. It seems a relative appeared and claims Carter died, making him the heir."

Weston smiled. "How interesting. I daresay you filed the legal papers before his death, so the relative has no case."

Another question to ask the lawyer.

"Furthermore, Peter, I have a project I'm anxious to start. If we close the loan this week, I shall add a three percent bonus. I'm sure that would be welcome."

"I'll discuss the legal issue with my lawyer and get in touch with you as soon as I can."

LATER THAT DAY
JANE'S BEDROOM

Despite Jane holding her hand, Mary Beth lay on the bed and worried. Dr. Smith stood on the other side of the bed, examining her, a solemn expression lining his face. Mary Beth's chest and throat ached with an intensity that frightened her. She regretted her trip to the Harden home, especially now that the doctor was looking down her throat. He must know. He must be furious. After returning from their excursion, she and Jane snuck back into the bedroom without even seeing a maid. Obviously, the outing worsened her condition.

Dr. Smith gazed into her eyes. "Mary Beth, how do you feel compared to yesterday?"

"It hurts more." Should she tell him how severely it hurt or keep that a secret? Either way she wouldn't give the details of her jaunt. She didn't want him to tell her father or Elsie. "Is that unusual?"

"In some cases. The first twenty-four hours is often the worst." He opened his black bag and put away his tools.

"Has it been twenty-four hours?"

Jane nodded. "Almost."

"How is my father?"

Dr. Smith glared at Mary Beth. "I have him well in hand."

"I want to see him as soon as possible When can he return to work?"

The doctor cleared his throat. "I expected you to improve more by this time, so I am going to extend your stay here another day, maybe two. I do not want you to leave this room."

The doctor didn't answer her question. Was he holding back information? The possibility terrified her. "Will that help?"

"Yes. Activity puts a strain on already irritated tissues." He held up a bottle. "Jane, see that she takes this additional medicine three times a day. Follow the instructions and mix in water."

"Yes, doctor." Jane took the bottle.

Mary Beth held in a groan. If only she could have interviewed Mrs. Harden. So much needed to be done.

TWO DAYS LATER
NOON

The air was humid and oppressive when Peter headed toward the bank from the café across the street. He had stopped in for pastries for his own staff. Everyone was working so hard to assist him, and he wanted to reward their efforts, just as Mr. Roper would do. Carrying a cloth-covered basket, he would leave the food with Mr. Riddle and hurry to his next appointment.

"Mr. Chandler, I went to your house to arrest you." A voice came from behind Peter.

Peter broke out in a sweat as the sheriff grabbed his arm. Everything about the sheriff, from his dark eyes to his protruding muscles and towering figure, intimidated him.

"Good morning," Peter said, chuckling. Surely the man was joking.

"You fall within the age range for conscription in the Confederate military and have not obeyed the law." The sheriff's deep voice growled.

Peter groaned. He didn't have time for this. "I know nothing about that, but I signed up with the militia to protect the city."

"You are under arrest."

"No." Peter pulled away, trying to balance the basket without losing its contents. "I cannot disappear without telling my employees. Mr. Roper is ill."

"You should've thought of that." The sheriff dragged him down the street away from the bank.

Peter saw the chubby figure of Mr. Grant coming toward the bank. Typical of Grant, he looked straight ahead, most likely focused on his own thoughts. "Please. There's my bank manager. I have to talk to him."

The sheriff kept going.

"Mr. Grant!" Peter waved, dropping the basket. He looked behind him and saw the pastries littering the wooden sidewalk. "Mr. Grant!"

"Hush, or I shall also charge you with resisting arrest."

The sheriff hurried down the street to a small building which served as city hall. He took him to the jail and shoved him into a cell. "You can stay here until you have complied."

Utterly ridiculous. If Peter ever got out, he would file a complaint with the judge. "How am I supposed to comply in here?"

"That's your problem." The sheriff smugly stomped away.

Peter shouted until he was hoarse for the sheriff to come back. How could he communicate from here? Or manage the bank? What would his mother think? She would worry when he didn't come home.

CHAPTER THIRTEEN

JANE'S BEDROOM
THE SAME DAY

Feeling much better, Mary Beth had graduated to sitting in an overstuffed chair beside the bed with a light blanket over her legs. She still experienced discomfort, and she was determined to rest even though her mind needed activity. Jane had situated her so she could gaze out the window at the sunshine and see bushes and trees which separated the Haskell property and her father's. She had sent a servant to find the doctor with an urgent request to see her father. The doctor's reluctance to speak of his illness greatly worried her.

Jane opened the door and peeked in, smiling. "Are you dressed?"

"Yes, and I do hope you have good news."

Jane stepped inside, shutting the door with her body. "The doctor did not agree because he needs to see you first. However, Maud brought fresh muffins, and Ida came to see you. So ... I asked cook to make tea, if you don't mind," she said.

"Of course." An impromptu chat sounded perfect. She would try to learn more about the mob at the bank since Peter and her father weren't able to. The sooner they found the culprit who killed Mr. Harden, the better.

Jane opened the door wide and spoke into the hall,

"You may come in."

Several ladies, wearing white aprons, came in and set up a small round tea table in the dressing area across from the bed. Ida also floated in wearing a new frock of ice pink.

"Ida, you look lovely." Mary Beth thought about how sad she must look in comparison.

"And you appear quite well, except for pallor. From Dr. Smith's description, I thought you must be near death."

Mary Beth recalled how much she ached after her impulsive trip to Mrs. Harden's house. "I thought I might …"

Ida frowned. "Might what?"

"Die."

"Really? Dreadful. I apologize." A tight smile spread over Ida's face as she eased into a chair one of the servants placed by the table. "Oh … my favorite muffins."

Servants continued setting up with tea, plates, and muffins near Mary Beth.

A servant curtsied. "Anything else?"

"Not now." Jane waved a dismissive hand and chose a chair on the other side of the table, serving both ladies.

"Our cook is wonderful." Mary Beth gulped down hot tea and shuddered as her mouth hurt. She didn't need more burns. She turned to Ida for information since her father was sheriff. Ida often overheard her father discussing issues with his deputies. "I haven't been out in several days. Any more unrest?"

"My father has been very uneasy," Ida said. She spooned sugar in her tea. "According to him, tempers are much too hot in town, and he kept me home several days."

"Were you out that day, Jane?" Mary Beth toyed with her muffin. Her appetite hadn't returned and burning her mouth didn't help. "I am wondering who might have seen the crowd, because I came later."

"Mother and I were shopping in town that morning, but we came home before the ruckus started," Jane said.

"I know Mrs. Nelson was there." Ida sipped her tea. "She spoke of one man who seemed to start the whole thing."

How interesting. "Did she know the person's name?"

Ida reached for her second muffin. "Not likely. If she had, I daresay she would tell everyone. She said the printer was there. Of course, he was not the one upsetting people, and the man who sells railroad tickets joined the crowd."

Mary Beth made a mental note of that. If she could talk to the man at the ticket counter, he might remember more. "Do you recall his name?"

"He has dark hair and talks fast."

"I am seeing Confederate soldiers around. From the train, maybe?" Jane said. "Would you like more milk in your tea, Mary Beth?"

"Yes." Milk would bring the temperature down. "Thanks. Did your father request the soldiers, Ida?"

"I don't think so. He mentioned they can be unruly too." Ida closed her eyes and grinned. "We need more attractive soldiers in town. Have you asked Peter to dinner yet? He's so handsome."

"No. He hasn't been to dinner, but he has come to talk with Papa."

Ida giggled. "So that's his excuse."

"I am not on Peter's mind," Mary Beth said.

From the look on Ida's face, she didn't appear to agree, and Ida would tease her without mercy later.

Chattanooga Jail
5:00 a.m.
The Following Morning

Clang! Clang! Peter rubbed his eyes while sitting up, and his feet made a dull sound as they banged the stone floor. The board he'd been lying on was a poor excuse for a bed. In the darkness, he could almost make out the bars of his cell, and he hoped the sound meant the sheriff had relented. He inhaled the odor of mold as a light appeared down the hallway to his left.

"Peter?" Dr. Smith's voice came from the end of the hall.

Peter's heart pummeled his chest. What was the doctor doing here? It must be the middle of the night, but Peter couldn't see his watch. "I am here."

"Sheriff gave me keys, which I intend to keep a while if he intends locking up innocent civilians. He has grown weary with people who favor the North. Troublemakers, he calls them," the doctor said, as he came closer. He held a lighted candle and a round metal holder with skeleton keys. The light flickered over his thin, bearded face.

"Not me," Peter said. "And the rest of the place appears empty."

"Exactly." Smith arrived at Peter's cell door. "Besides, the city needs a banker."

"How did you find me?" Peter asked.

"Your mother contacted Mr. Riddle, who said you would be visiting clients and working late in the office. That satisfied her until she woke and found you still gone.

She sent for me, and I alerted the sheriff, who was asleep."

Peter laughed. "You got him out of bed. I suppose that's my vengeance, although right now, I'd love to punch the man."

"Yes. I would say you are avenged. I shall talk to the city council about an exemption from military service given the circumstances." Smith turned the key, and the hinges squealed as he swung open the door. "You best get home to your mother. It's almost dawn, and she's quite upset."

Peter ran home to calm his mother. Banking problems could wait.

THE ROPER HOME
9:00 A.M.

Mary Beth stood at her father's bedside, holding his hand. He lay on his side, and the brilliant brocade bedspread tucked around him emphasized the whiteness of his skin. His raspy breathing and lethargy sent chills through her body. No wonder the doctor would not reveal her father's condition while she recovered. Papa was much worse than she had imagined, despite the doctor's warnings. She sank to her knees and kissed his forehead. "Papa, I love you."

"Mary Beth, your bed is ready," Jane came to her side.

If she lost Papa, she would lose her mother all over again since he could relate stories of a mother she barely remembered. "I cannot leave him. What if—"

"Dr. Smith made you promise to rest after we moved you back." Jane tugged at her arm. "He will be here soon, and I will be in trouble."

"You are right." Dr. Smith walked in. With one brow

cocked, he led Mary Beth toward the door. "You are in trouble."

With a backward glance at her father, she relented. The doctor had promised she would be well soon. Until then, she would gather information from visitors—now that she could have them—about the bank murder. "Papa looks terrible."

He led her down the hall to her bedroom on the left past the stairs. "If you recall, I alerted you. Rest now. I shall be here when you wake."

Mary Beth stretched out on her bed without turning down the pink bedspread as Dr. Smith closed her door. How could she sleep with her father so ill? If she prayed and prayed, maybe everything would be all right.

Two Days Later
C&R Bank

Peter rose from his desk and offered his hand to the elderly councilman who stood in the office doorway. Would the clutter on his desk convince the man he needed to work rather than sit in jail? "Please come in, sir."

"Aye." The gray-headed man inched into Peter's office. He had a paunch protruding from his coat, a very white beard, and an outdated tie.

Peter examined the man's impassive face for any sign of his thoughts. Surely the doctor's recommendation would be enough to establish his need for an exemption from military service. "May we fetch you fresh tea?"

"Nah." The man hobbled over the desk, adjusted his glasses, and gazed at a file there. "You have a mess here.

What is all this about an exemption?"

Peter ambled around the desk and pulled the file from the councilman's fingers. Instead he handed the councilman a note containing the latest threats from the sheriff who warned of more imprisonment. "If you read this, it should explain. As for the exemption, Mr. Roper had a severe heart attack and cannot work. Should I go back in prison, the bank would be forced to close."

"Indeed?" The man's bushy brows puckered. "Roper is much too young for such an illness."

Peter hoped the city council did not expect him to share facts about the illness. His first imprisonment had upset his mother so much he feared for her health. And he detested the way she hovered over him as if he were a child. "Is there anything else you need?"

"I shall present this to the full council and call for a vote. According to the city charter, a vote of this kind must be approved by all the members."

"Do you have any idea when you will make a final decision?" The sheriff had allowed him two more days.

"Decision?" The man groaned as he pulled himself to his feet. "Surely we can agree before the war ends."

"Excuse me?" Peter was horrified.

"You young 'uns keep saying the war should not last long. So, it may not matter."

"I need an exemption as soon as possible." He would visit each member in the evenings and explain the situation—if he must.

"We shall see." The man frowned as he shuffled out.

Peter groaned under his breath.

CHAPTER FOURTEEN

Briefcase in hand, Peter's steps slowed as he neared the picket fence outside the Roper home. He didn't want to bother Mr. Roper, nor did he want to interact with Mary Beth, but Mr. Weston requested the bank close on the Carter property this week. In light of Mr. Owen's threats, he needed his partner's advice. Plus, his lawyer had advised him to obtain a power of attorney from Roper for bank business. A clerk from the lawyer's office would meet him here.

Peter opened the gate and walked down the gravel path to the front door. As he climbed the steps to the porch, Mary Beth stepped out. "Hello, Peter. What brings you to see us?"

He didn't meet her eyes. "I apologize, but I must speak to your father, briefly."

Mary Beth opened the front door and moved out of his way. "He has been awake more today. I hope you are brief."

"I plan to be." Peter wished Maud had come to the door. He didn't want to lapse into their old friendship. He must treat her as a mere friend, an acquaintance rather than with the intensity that burned inside. "How is Eddie? I have not seen him since I returned."

"He is dead."

"What?" He stood motionless in the hallway. Horrible

response. He wanted to swallow his tongue. "I am terribly sorry ..."

"Don't be." Her green eyes blazed, highlighting the slight pallor in her cheeks. "Eddie womanized, and I hate that."

"He hurt you." The words came unbidden, but he expected Eddie to do just that. At the same time, he hated the man for treating her that way. "He deserves ..."

Mary Beth nodded. "Thank you for being angry. I feel justified."

Peter knotted his hands into fists, realizing he would have to forgive Eddie since God had already judged him. "Please accept my apologies. I understand you were injured in your father's accident. I should have dropped by sooner—"

"Dr. Smith kept visitors away for several days." She led him to the sitting room. "So, please do not trouble yourself with another apology."

Peter swallowed a laugh as she demonstrated the same compassion she did when they were growing up. She looked exhausted, and if he laughed now, she'd be annoyed. However, her announcement about Eddie changed him from a competitor to friend again, and he liked that.

"I have made progress on the mob, despite my ... accident." She continued.

They worked well with each other, and he hoped she could turn up something. Maybe he could convince her not to search for the murderer. "Actually, I have a job that might be more useful right now."

Her green eyes glowed. "What do you need?"

Peter, with Mary Beth beside him, stood in the bedroom where Mr. Roper lay abed with his eyes closed, wearing a white nightshirt with blankets up to his chest. Heavy damask drapes kept out the morning light, and except for the odor of medication, the atmosphere resembled a wake rather than a sick room. His stomach recoiled as he peered into Mr. Roper's whitened face. His partner looked close to death. "Mr. Roper?"

No response.

Mary Beth tugged at Peter's arm, whispering, "Do *not* upset him. Doctor's orders."

A lump formed in his throat as he tried to decide what to do. He longed for guidance, but he couldn't harm Mr. Roper or unsettle Mary Beth. "Sir?"

"How odd. He's been awake this morning." She leaned over and stroked her father's face. "Papa?"

Mr. Roper opened glazed eyes. "My girl."

"Peter came to see you." She nodded toward Peter. "See?"

"How's the bank?"

Peter moved forward preparing to ask a question.

"Be careful," Mary Beth leaned close to whisper, "No ... bad news."

Based on Mary Beth's frown and his partners weakness, Peter's errand seemed useless. "Do you have any instructions for me?"

Roper mumbled.

Peter leaned closer. "Excuse me."

Roper's voice was breathy. "Continue what I taught you."

"I will, sir."

"You've exhausted him." She pulled him from the bed.

"No harm done if you leave now." Dr. Smith walked in, and his eyes narrowed as he moved toward Mr. Roper. He waved a finger under Mary Beth's nose. "I want you to go outside in the fresh air. In fact, I think you and Jane should drive to see Mrs. Harden soon. She has just recovered from illness and needs the company."

"But—" Mary Beth held up a hand.

"I shall watch over your father." Dr. Smith raised both brows. "I want you well enough to start learning how to care for him."

"Don't forget my errand." Peter wanted Mary Beth to forget about the murder.

Mary Beth, accompanied by Jane, headed downtown to the bank to follow up on Peter's request. The fresh, warm air and exercise invigorated her more than she expected. She had been afraid her lungs would ache the way they had the day she'd visited the Harden home, but she had improved a lot. She waved at an acquaintance who walked into the butcher shop and nodded at people from church as they clattered along the dusty streets.

"How long will it take you to find the contract?" Jane adjusted her bonnet and re-tied the ribbons.

"Not long." Mary Beth shrugged. "If Mr. Riddle cannot find the contract, Papa must have left it in his office. That's where I plan to look."

"My errand is quite short."

"Ah, then I will work fast." Mary Beth reached the bank door and opened it, hearing the bell chime above the door.

Mr. Grant stood by the door. "Welcome, Miss Roper.

Miss Haskell, how can I help you?"

"I have a deposit." Jane handed a parcel to Mr. Grant.

"Right this way." He waved toward the teller window.

Mary Beth left Jane and hurried up the stairs in the back of the foyer. Once on the landing she turned left into the bank office and left again to her father's door, which she unlocked. Her father's desk looked like it did when he left for the day. He had piled all his work on the table behind his desk. She hurried to his files and looked through each one. Nothing appeared with Mr. Carter's name, even when she went through the desk drawers. Where had her father placed the file? Peter said her father had it when Mr. Owen came the first time. If he sued as Peter expected, they would need to know the provisions of the agreement.

FOUR DAYS LATER

Bright sunshine heated the afternoon air as Peter and Mr. Weston stood outside Mr. Haskell's office where they had signed papers. A bumblebee buzzed around a planter filled with yellow petunias on the porch before it flew toward Peter. He moved away from the bee and toward the sidewalk, on his way to the bank.

"I appreciate your business," Weston offered a hand.

Peter shook his hand, conscious of the sums he held in his briefcase after completing the sale of the Carter property. "Thank you."

The two men parted with smiles and Peter strode to the bank, anxious to get the gold into the safe, the bumblebee still hovering around Peter's face even though he tried waving it off.

What a relief to reach the bank where he could shut the annoying bee outside and run up to his office. He settled into his chair and pulled out the papers to file.

Mr. Riddle walked in with his lips pressed together, carrying another stack of documents.

"Oh, good. Mr. Riddle." Peter handed him the new contract. "We just closed the loan with Mr. Weston. Could you file these?"

"Oh, yes, sir." He placed the document he held on Peter's desk. "Sir, the bank manager received this while you were out. I believe these are legal papers."

"Who sent them?" Peter sat down to read, hoping this was not the lawsuit Owen had promised.

"I believe the lawyer named Mr. James." Riddle stepped away from the door. "Is there anything else you need?"

"No. But thanks." Peter's stomach swirled and sickened as he flipped through the legal papers Mr. James had filed on behalf of Mr. Owen. He chose to sue the bank for $21,000, which meant the bank would fold if they lost.

ROPER LIBRARY
LATE THAT EVENING

Mary Beth struck a match and lit the oil lamp on her father's desk which splattered light so she could read. She didn't like examining her father's belongings, but with a lawsuit threatened, Peter needed Carter's contract. She inhaled the lingering odor of smoke and her chest tightened. Memories slammed into her mind—her father slumped over the desk, fire blazing, and stomping out the flames. Her throat tingled, and she coughed.

She reached for a stack of papers on the corner of the desk and sifted through them. The butcher's bill sat on top, then a letter from her uncle, and then a novel by Mary Shelley with her mother's name written inside the cover. Why would her father be reading that book? Next, she unfolded a short letter her father had started writing describing the pain in his shoulder. He commented the doctor had warned him such pain could mean a heart attack. Terrible! He knew and continued working.

Maud knocked on the door and walked in. "I be a tellin' you your father has been coughin' for ten minutes now. I never heard such a noise in all my life and I knowed you would want me to be a tellin' you."

Mary Beth groaned and ran upstairs. The contract would have to wait.

CHAPTER FIFTEEN

THREE DAYS LATER

Once again, Mary Beth, accompanied by Jane, rode toward the Harden's house. She gazed out at the overcast skies trying to decide how to start the conversation. Her father knew the family, but she had never met them. Dr. Smith had said Mrs. Harden had a daughter in her twenties, and Mary Beth would like to be friends with her.

"I wonder who lives in that house?" Jane nodded toward a white house with freshly cut lawn.

"Could that be Carter's property?" Mary Beth leaned across her friend to look out the window on Jane's side. "Did we see that last time?"

"We did not. But the groom is bringing us in the opposite way." Jane leaned back in the seat.

The carriage stopped in front of the Harden house and Mary Beth hopped out, waiting for Jane.

Boom!

"What was that?" Mary Beth looked around. The Harden home and the Carter home sat about two miles apart. Farmland stretched in each direction.

"Get back inside." The groom yelled. "Someone fired a gun."

Jane's eyes widened. She froze in the carriage doorway.

Bang! The smell of black powder filled the air with

another explosion.

"Let's go!" The groom shouted.

Trembling, Mary Beth pushed Jane inside and lunged in afterward. The carriage sped down the road, veering left and right. Jane squealed.

The girls sat hunched down while the groom yelled at the horses to go faster.

Peter tugged at his collar as he glanced around his office. Piles of documents covered his desk and the floor beside. A few also sat on the bookcase beside the door. His father would never tolerate such clutter, especially when a client would be visiting soon. Being thrown into the job didn't give him time to organize. He was writing a reply to a letter that was missing.

He located a stack of mail Riddle had handed him earlier in the week and flipped through the contents.

Mr. Riddle dashed in his office. "Excuse me, sir, you have a message from the Roper family. Miss Roper asked for you right away."

His heart descended in protest. Mr. Roper must be worse. He couldn't imagine what he would do if … but he must not let fear take over. "I cannot find the letter from Savannah. Please search for me. I shall be at the Roper's home. Thank you."

He raced out the door and through town, hoping he wouldn't be seeing his partner for the last time. By the time he reached the home, he was out of breath and sweaty.

Maud opened the door as Peter stepped through the white picket fence. "We's so glad to be a seein' you. What an uproar we been havin', I wished I'm a never. Them Union men may be attackin', and I sure be a hopin' not. For heaven's sake, I ain't sure what to do."

He hurried toward the house, more worried than ever. "What is going on?"

Her face blanched in terror, Mary Beth burst into the foyer and blurted out how someone fired guns at them. She pulled him into the sitting room where Jane sat on the sofa.

Jane's face was white. "I would have called my father, but he's in Cleveland today for a case."

Peter sighed, imagining the danger. He needed facts, and he turned to Mary Beth, hoping she hadn't tried to solve the murder. "Where were you? And why?"

"Jane and I attempted to see Mrs. Harden again. My dad said I should."

"Attempted to see her? Does that mean you didn't?"

"The groom heard gunshots." Jane's voice shook.

"I've never seen him drive so fast." Mary Beth collapsed on the sofa beside Jane. "Somehow, I think we're close to solving the murder."

Maud knocked on the door and guided the sheriff inside.

"Solving what murder?" The sheriff's huge face wore displeasure. His enormous frame towered over Mary Beth.

"Mr. Harden's." Mary Beth shrank into the cushions.

"That's my job. Not yours." He glanced at Peter. "And here you are again. Do you have that exemption yet?"

"I do. In my office." Peter folded his arms and met the sheriff's gaze.

"It belongs in my office, or I shall take you back to jail." He turned to Mary Beth and Jane. "Did you call me to say you've been looking for a murderer?"

Mary Beth took a deep breath. "No. We heard gunshots."

The sheriff pulled a pad of paper from his shirt pocket. "Did you see a man shooting?"

"No," Jane said.

Mary Beth shook her head.

"Did you see anyone injured?" The sheriff's face hardened.

Mary Beth looked at Jane who shook her head. "No."

"Where did this happen? The sheriff wrote on his pad.

"They went to the Harden's home." Peter eased toward Mary Beth. He didn't like the murderous glare the sheriff directed toward her.

"Were you there too?" The sheriff bellowed.

"No. I work at the bank." Peter was hot.

"Keep it that way." The sheriff's chest expanded as he turned to Jane and Mary Beth. "I want you two ladies to go back to your knitting."

Peter agreed they should stop looking for a murderer, but he was still worried about Mary Beth. He moved toward the door. "We should call for Dr. Smith to look over these ladies."

Dr. Smith walked into the room. "They are fine, Peter. I came to see Mr. Roper when the girls returned and examined them. Other than being shaken, they sustained no injuries. But I did send for the sheriff."

"Both of you are safe, so stop worrying." The sheriff put away his notes. "We are in a war in which soldiers shoot guns. You probably came across Northern scouts. If you stay home, where you belong, you should be safe."

"You aren't going to investigate?" Mary Beth's face

turned red.

"He'll do his job." Peter said, nodding toward the sheriff.

"What's to investigate?" The sheriff crossed his arms. "They didn't see anyone with a gun or anyone hurt. I think we have a couple hysterical women who should mind their own business."

"What?" Peter wanted to punch the sheriff, but he wouldn't because his father taught him better manners. Mary Beth wasn't hysterical. "I think you should look into this situation."

"You heard me." The sheriff stamped his way to the door. "I have real work to do."

Dr. Smith raised both hands. "I shall go investigate if no one else will."

Apparently, someone had threatened Mary Beth and Jane. Peter could give up the bank, but he would not allow anyone to hurt Mary Beth. Someone had to unravel this mess if the sheriff wouldn't. "I shall assist you."

"You will need Papa's rifles. He has several," Mary Beth said, rushing toward the door. "And I must accompany you because we never got a chance to talk to Mrs. Harden."

Jane's face turned whiter. "I shall stay home and pray."

Peter took Mary Beth's arm. "I wish you would stay with Jane. Prayer would be the best response."

Mary Beth's green eyes flashed in anger. "I shall pray *and* go with you."

THIRTY MINUTES LATER

Peter rode his horse toward Carter's property alongside the carriage which held Mary Beth and Dr. Smith. The doctor had insisted on driving the carriage in case he had a patient to bring back. Mary Beth had promised to stay inside until he made sure they faced no danger.

Peter's gaze swept the landscape. The skies were gray, but birds sang, and a light breeze blew as they passed corn fields and cotton. As the group neared Carter's property, Peter's heart sped up. He pulled in front of Carter's property, secured his horse at the wooden fence, and loaded his rifle.

Rifle in hand, Smith came alongside. "We should advance slowly and stay covered."

Peter moved toward the house beside Smith, noticing the trimmed lawn offered no debris to hide behind. If the shooter was still armed, he and Dr. Smith might have to run fast for cover.

The front door slammed open. Mr. Weston stumbled out, hands raised and slid into a half-sitting position. He wore no coat, and blood covered his left side. "I am unarmed. Did someone ... alert law enforcement?"

Peter lowered his gun. "Mr. Weston. We don't have the sheriff with us, but I brought Dr. Smith. An eyewitness heard shots fired."

"Correct. Whoever did this ... also fired on my men ... while they cleaned up the property. This time I got my gun ... and defended myself," Weston said, breathing hard.

"I shall get my medical case from the carriage. Anyone else wounded?" Smith said.

"Dead."

The doctor shook his head as he stalked to the carriage.

Peter picked up his gun, readying to search. "How long ago did this happen?"

"I … cannot say. He got … my shoulder … at least twice. I may have passed out …" Weston leaned against the doorframe grimacing. "Death threats … came but I assumed … pranks. I guess."

"Take death threats seriously." Smith arrived with his black bag. "Let me help you in and take care of those wounds."

"It's pretty deserted out here except for that house." Peter nodded toward the Harden home in the distance. "And her husband was recently murdered. Do you know who was shooting?"

"No. But whomever it was is in the field behind my house, somewhere. Get him off my land. Please." Weston pleaded as Dr. Smith helped him back into the house.

Peter wandered along the property, searching under bushes and behind trees. Several hundred yards from the house, he found a body behind a thick shrub. Mr. Carter. Peter couldn't believe it. Mr. Owen had claimed he was already dead. That would make it hard to obtain a death certificate. However, Carter had two gunshots, one in the chest and one in the head. His mouth hung open, and blood had drained from his mouth onto the dirt. His eyes stared at nothing.

Peter's stomach churned. He moved several feet away and left his breakfast in the tall weeds.

CHAPTER SIXTEEN

Caw. Caw. Caw.

Mary Beth yawned and stretched, realizing she had fallen asleep in the carriage sitting in front of the Carter home. The doctor had returned for his bag to treat a man in Carter's old home. He told her to rest since she was still recovering. But she felt fine, except for lingering fatigue. The white house looked partially painted, and a pile of new brick sat beside the ramshackle fireplace. Neither Dr. Smith nor Peter were in sight. Was it safe to wander out? She opened the carriage door to step out on freshly cut lawn just as the sound of footsteps startled her. Ducking behind the open door, she realized the material might not protect her from gunfire.

Cough.

She peeked around the door. Peter, his face ashen, bent over beside the fireplace gagging. He pulled out a handkerchief and mopped his face.

"Are you okay?" she shouted. What disaster caused that reaction? She hurried toward him as a lump formed in her throat.

"No." He swayed. "He's dead."

"Who?" Her heart pounded.

"I found Carter's body." Peter sighed.

"What?"

"I'm going for the sheriff," Peter said.

Peter guided the sheriff inside the living area of Carter's old house. Wide-eyed, Mary Beth sat on a nearby overstuffed chair that appeared new. Weston lay on the sofa swathed in bandages, and Dr. Smith hovered nearby. The room was clean, and crates of all sizes lay scattered about the room.

The doctor rose. "Morning, Sheriff. Mr. Weston is in here. The shooter, Mr. Carter, is lying several yards behind the house."

The sheriff scowled. "I can do my own investigation, sir. And I'm still not convinced I shouldn't put Peter Chandler in jail."

"No. You are overreacting to all the upheaval in town." Dr. Smith walked between them. "Besides, we've talked about Peter."

"I heard you, but I could use some people in my empty cells." He pointed to Mr. Weston. "Why are you here? I thought you had a home on Lookout Mountain."

Peter explained how the bank foreclosed on the property and sold it to Weston, who intended to build a profitable farm.

The sheriff turned to Weston. "Explain what happened."

"I received several threatening notes when I started repairing and upgrading the house," Weston said. "But I didn't take them seriously."

"Amazing. You don't bother to tell me until someone gets shot?" the sheriff puffed out his chest.

"I have several men working here, and they play jokes on each other." Weston winced as he tried to sit up. "You'll find the notes on the table in the kitchen.

"I shall fetch them." Peter walked into the adjoining room, which boasted a rustic table, cookstove and sink. Assorted papers lay on the table. He grabbed them and shoved them into the sheriff's hand.

"Yeah!" The sheriff examined the notes. "If you'd told me about these, we might not have a dead body out back. Which reminds me, Mr. Weston, are you joining up for the war effort?"

"No. I am past the age for mandatory subscription. I can shoot, but I doubt I could keep up with those boys marching."

The sheriff scowled. "I need to know exactly when the letters started and what happened today."

Weston explained.

"Let me understand, Mr. Weston. The man was shooting at you, and you fired back. Somewhere in there, he injured you, and you killed him. Mr. Chandler, you came here because Miss Roper and Miss Haskell heard gunshots. You found Mr. Carter dead. And this man was supposed to be dead already?" A scowl covered the sheriff's ruddy face.

Peter nodded. He couldn't help recalling the sheriff didn't want to investigate the gun shots the girls reported. "Carter's body is outside. I found a gun beside his body."

"What a mess," The sheriff said. "From now on stay out of my business. All of you. Let me do my job."

Peter suspected the mess had not ended yet.

MR. GRAY'S OFFICE

Mary Beth settled into a comfortable chair in the almost empty waiting room at Peter's lawyer's office, thankful she had finally located Carter's contract in her father's desk drawer. She had handed the document to the secretary at the front desk when she came in. Hopefully, the lawyer could devise a strategy to fight Owen's lawsuit. Not many women carried on business, but she saw herself filling in for her father. After his death, she would own almost half the bank. Besides, Peter had so much to do running the bank alone he had requested her assistance.

Her thoughts strayed back to events of the past few days. Peter's restraints had fallen away since she had explained the situation with Eddie. She didn't expect them to be a couple, but she often longed for a return to their old friendship. The change excited her.

Mr. Gray's secretary motioned for her to enter the lawyer's office, where a vague odor of paper and ink tickled her nose. Mr. Gray sat at his desk in front of a huge bookcase examining a book. He looked up and yanked off his glasses. "Oh, good morning. I have very good news. The plaintiff in this suit has no case."

"What?" She never expected to hear this. "I thought ..."

"The sale contract clearly states you have the right to repossess if the purchaser does not pay his bill for five months. Even if you set that aside, you have no death certificate to prove the original owner died."

"Carter only died yesterday. I saw the body." A shiver streaked up her spine as she recalled the men who carried Carter off the property. "Now that he is dead, does that change our position?"

"How long ago did Mr. Owen file the suit?" Mr. Gray

asked.

"Last week." Mary Beth held her breath.

"That sounds like fraud, which makes your case even stronger. Not many people get confused over whether or not their relative is dead."

Mary Beth had read part of the document while sitting with her father, but she didn't understand the legal language. From now on, Peter would keep track of all the contracts, at least until her father recovered. She sighed with relief as the lawyer stood, closing their interview. "What do you advise now?"

"Contact Owen and ask him to drop the suit," Mr. Gray said. "If he doesn't, you can charge him with harassment and fraud. To do that you would need to contact the sheriff."

The sheriff. Peter might not enjoy dealing with him again. "I shall tell Peter he can do that. He may want to talk to you first."

"I would be delighted to help." Mr. Gray escorted her to the door. "Ask the secretary out front for a schedule of fees. These can be quite expensive if we charge by the hour."

Expensive? Mary Beth wasn't sure what her father would say about an extended court case while he was sick. Would Peter know? They'd best clear this up right away.

CHAPTER SEVENTEEN

Peter sat at his desk studying a contract. A potential client with the railroad had submitted an alternative contract to the bank's typical agreement. He weighed the alternatives, trying to understand how much the changes would impact the bank.

A noise at his office door caught his attention.

His mother stood in the door. Her shawl hung unevenly, as if she had donned it in a hurry, and her face was wet with tears. "Peter!"

"Mama?" The last few days she had been calmer, and he thought she was adjusting to his schedule. "What's wrong?"

"You did not come home, and it's getting late." She swiped a hand across her cheek as she hurried in and plopped into a wingback chair in front of his desk.

Peter pulled his pocket watch out. It was 6:30, and the bank was closed. His mother must have used her key. "I haven't stayed any later than usual. What brought you here?"

Tears streamed down her face. "Are you taking precautions for your safety?"

"What?" Some new issue must be bothering her.

She took a deep breath. "I had a dream, and I can't ..."

A dream? She was fine when he left for work this morning. "Last night? When?"

"You have to understand I haven't slept normally since ... your father died." She dabbed at her tears with a damp handkerchief. "And Ruthie has been upset since you ... took your father's place at the table."

"Mama. I don't have to sit there." Peter strode around his desk and put a hand on her shoulder.

"She's just upset, Peter. We had a particularly sharp argument after you left for work. She's just so uneasy." His mother took a deep breath. "This afternoon, I sat down to read, to distract my mind. I fell asleep."

"But that's good." Peter pulled up a straight chair so he could sit beside her. "You finally rested."

"No." She shook her head, and her lips trembled. "I dreamed your father was dying. I could see the bed, but I couldn't walk fast enough to get to him. Finally, I reached his side and saw his face ... it was your face. You breathed your last. I saw it."

"But I'm fine." Peter took her hands. "There's nothing to worry about."

"I couldn't move even though I could see you. It was awful." She sobbed.

His eyes filled with tears as he held her hands. "It was a dream, that is all. I am not in danger."

His mother's weeping waned. "I'm so sorry to bother you.

"You came to me, and that's what I want you to do."

"Your father hasn't been gone long, and I can easily lose perspective. I'm so sorry." She took his hands and squeezed. "But please be careful."

He must agree. At this moment she wasn't oppressing

him with concern, but she might still do that, particularly with this loss. "Of course."

"Thank you." She released his hands and sat back in the chair.

Peter walked to his desk. "Let me organize a few things, and we can walk home together."

"I'd like that." She smiled and rushed toward him, embracing him.

They both wept together."

THE NEXT MORNING
THE ROPER HOUSE

The air was cool and the sun beginning to rise as Peter opened the white picket gate to enter the Roper property. He had to discover what Mary Beth had learned from the lawyer. No doubt she would come to him soon, but he couldn't wait. And banking demanded so much time, working by himself. He passed the flowers along the walk and climbed the steps to knock on the door.

Maud opened the door. "I be ... I not be expectin' you, but you be always welcome. I be a runnin' upstairs to get Mary Beth bein' sure she be fully ... dressed if you know what I mean."

"Sorry, Maud. I didn't give you warning."

"Never be a mindin', dear boy. I shall be a seeing to her." She took his arm and led him into the sitting room. "Jus' sit yerself down on the sofa there, and she be a comin' soon."

Peter eased into the brocade cushions of the sofa, wondering if he'd done right coming so early. His mother's tears motivated him to clear up the mystery about the Carter property. He knew of no danger, but she and his father started the bank together. She still felt responsible and any bank crisis would upset her further.

About ten minutes later, Mary Beth entered. Her face was pink, and her hair was down, fluffy around her shoulders. A light blue dress accentuated her fair complexion. "Good morning."

"Sorry for—"

"Nonsense." She grinned and sat on the other end of the couch. "You are practically family."

Not exactly what he hoped for, but that was all in the past. "I came to find out what the lawyer said and to clear up the mess. Did you find the contract?" He leaned toward her.

"Yes. And the lawyer said Owen had no case." She explained what the lawyer told her.

"I'll find the lawyer and request he drop the suit."

"We." She leaned toward him. "I can ask around, send some telegrams to Nashville."

"Promise me you will stay here. If you write the telegram, I shall send it. Message Crutchfield House asking if he's there."

"You should also take precautions. Owen worries me, especially after the gunfire at Carter's old house." She flattened her lips.

"My revolver." He patted his pocket. "I shall start to carry it. As a banker, that's not unusual."

THE NEXT EVENING

C&R Bank

Peter glanced at his watch as he dashed down the bank stairs. While organizing his work, he'd lost track of time. He could kick himself for being late again and making his mother worry.

Clang.

He stopped short. Keys? No one should be unlocking the bank door.

Mary Beth stepped in and secured the door behind her. "Peter. I came to see you."

"You've got information?" His heart sped up.

"Yes." She ran to him, holding up a telegram. "There's no lawyer in Nashville by that name."

"Oh." He took the paper and read it. "But the court sent papers. Come upstairs, and I shall find the document."

Inside his office he cast a glance at his father's portrait hanging on the wall behind the desk. What would he think of Peter now? He frantically searched for the papers. "The folder should be here."

"Wouldn't Mr. Riddle file it?" Mary Beth picked up a stack of folders on the desk and thumbed through them. "I shall search in his office."

Peter took a deep breath, trying to recall when he last saw the annoying papers as Mary Beth walked across the hall with some matches.

"You should not be here right now. It's getting dark. You won't be safe walking home." He called out. He ran his hand through his hair. Mary Beth shouldn't have come here this late.

She returned, holding a lighted candle aloft, and handed him several papers. "Here. Look for the law firm."

He snatched the papers and examined them in the light

of the lamp. "The Firm of Wilson, Walker, and James. The address is Forty-Four Vine Street. Now we know who to contact."

"It's a mistake, surely." Mary Beth put the candle on his desk. "Write that down. I shall try again tomorrow."

"Did you find Owen?" Peter asked as he reached for clean paper.

"No. I checked every hotel in town and in Nashville. Where does he live?"

"I don't recall." He dipped his pen and wrote out the address. "No. He never said."

"But we know this Mr. James lives in Nashville. I can send out a telegram to him. I wish we had his address."

Peter blotted his writing and handed it to her. "Let me give you several dollars from petty cash——"

"Oh. We have cash at home." She shook her head as she folded the paper and crammed it into her drawstring purse.

"But this is a bank expense." He picked up the candle and hurried across the hall to Riddle's desk. He opened the top right drawer and counted out change.

"Peter. We have money." She stood behind him.

He pressed the gold into her hand. "I shall walk you home."

"You don't have to." She shook her head.

"I insist." He would hate himself if something happened to her.

Mary Beth gazed into Peter's eyes as he held her hand closed around the coins. He was so close she could smell his shaving soap. His blue eyes radiated kindness and affection. What would people think? They would be walking around town as darkness fell. She inhaled and decided she didn't care.

"Let's go." Peter smiled.

Her heart flip-flopped. His eyes held such warmth. And he was so close. "Shouldn't … we blow out the lamp?"

"Yes." He dropped her hand and went across the hall where he extinguished the lamp.

Her cheeks burned. Did Peter notice her blush? She hurried downstairs still holding the candle.

Peter came down behind her, blew out the candle and ushered her out the door.

"Mr. Chandler, I must talk to you." The sheriff strode up as Peter locked the door.

She took Peter's arm to show her support. The sheriff's hostile tone left no doubt he was upset again.

"You have my exemption. What now?" Peter's face stiffened.

"I have a body and no next of kin." The sheriff crossed his bulky arms. "If you had communicated your concerns like you should have, I would have known this information."

"Let's step inside." Peter unlocked the door and ushered the two inside the empty foyer.

"You are referring to Mr. Carter?" Mary Beth said.

"Yes." The sheriff kept his eyes on Peter. "The city will have the expense of his burial. You should have contacted me when you had problems with this man. We need background information when a case opens."

"I have spent all day trying to locate Mr. Owen and the law firm who sued," Mary Beth said. "And I intend to continue."

"Mr. Owen? Lawsuit?" Sheriff's mouth fell open. "I have never heard about this. What is going on?"

Peter rubbed his jaw, recalling the event. "Well, basically, sir, Mr. Owen claimed Carter was dead and that he inherited the property. He filed suit last week."

"This Mr. Owen sued you before Carter died? That's fraud. I never heard of this either. This is a job for law enforcement. I'm going to have to find all these people."

"Why not ask Mrs. Harden?" Mary Beth said. "Mr. Harden seemed to know Carter well."

"Right now?" Peter frowned. "It's really late."

"Yes." The sheriff said. "We must resolve these crimes, and it's early enough that Mrs. Harden shouldn't be in bed."

Mary Beth sighed and hoped he was right.

CHAPTER EIGHTEEN

Peter took Mary Beth's arm and ushered her outside into growing darkness. The cool air refreshed him. Stores around him had already closed, and no pedestrians walked on the streets. He wanted to finish the interview and untangle the mystery before the hour grew later. His mother expected him to work late, but he had no desire to stretch her patience. While he locked the bank door the second time, the sheriff clomped down the sidewalk to the corner.

"Who is this coming to the bank?" the sheriff asked. "I believe this is your mother."

Peter turned to see his mother pull up in the buggy. He hoped she wasn't upset or didn't have an emergency. Nevertheless, he would be gracious. "Mama? What brings you here?"

"Ma'am, it's late for you to be in town," the sheriff said.

"I came to stay with my son until he returns home." Mrs. Chandler handed the reins to Peter.

"How are you?" Peter looped the reigns over the porch railings. "Is Ruth all right?"

"Yes and yes. Ruth is staying with a friend tonight."

Peter faced a dilemma. His mother wanted companionship which he wouldn't have much time for tonight. Yet, she didn't need to be involved in this situation. He prayed she would understand. "I—we have a bank … errand with Mrs. Harden."

"Use the buggy," she said. "Our house is on the way, so you can drop me at home."

Peter took a deep breath to defend his action before he realized what she had said. She wasn't upset or fearful, nor did she ask for a description of the errand. He didn't receive a scolding for working past banking hours, and she seemed happy for him to go. He held out his hand to Mary Beth. "I like that plan. Let's go."

THE HARDEN HOME
THIRTY MINUTES LATER

Her chest tight, Mary Beth stood at the front door of the Harden home with Peter beside her. She hated to bother the family this late, and she would give profuse apologies. They had hurried to get here before the sheriff, since he didn't seem to be the gentle type, and she wanted to make sure the widow understood they cared.

A young lady about Mary Beth's age answered the door. She had shoulder-length brown hair, light brown eyes, and a thin face. "Yes?"

Mary Beth noted the home didn't have the unusual smell like the first day she had come. She introduced them. "We are from the C&R Bank—"

"And we have come to talk to your mother about Carter and the crimes he committed." Peter said.

Mary Beth couldn't believe he interrupted her. Maybe it was because she used the bank name, but her family owned almost half of the assets. "We apologize for the hour … it's so late … but the sheriff is on his way. He tends to be … blunt."

"I'm Miss Beverly Harden." She opened the door wide into a hardwood foyer with large ferns beside the door. She motioned for them to enter. "I understand you brought cookies at your last visit, Miss Roper. My mother was so grateful, and I hoped you would return."

"Did she enjoy the cookies?" What a stupid question. When they had so many serious issues to cover, she asked about food.

"Wonderful. But I shall let Mama tell you." Beverly said as she led them upstairs and down a hall with thick carpet and oil paintings on the walls. "We adhere to the British tradition of having a sitting room on the first floor rather than the ground floor."

"So lovely," Mary Beth murmured. The house reminded her of European gentry.

"You mentioned the sheriff?" Beverly stopped and turned toward them. Her eyebrows pulled together.

"He's investigating the late Mr. Carter." Mary Beth said.

"*Late* Mr. Carter?" She cocked her head.

"Yes. I apologize to say he passed away. I know your parents were his friends. Shot." Peter cleared his throat "Terribly disturbing."

"Yes," Mary Beth nodded, examining Miss Harden's face for emotion. Peter had certainly been gentler giving the news than the sheriff.

Beverly paused and glanced at each of them as she opened the sitting room door. "Mama won't be grieving. But she can share why if she wishes. Please, go in."

Mary Beth and Peter walked into the sitting room that boasted light brown wood and gray-green furnishings centered around a huge stone fireplace. A slim lady with light brown curls sat on a sofa surrounded by pillows in shades of gray and brown. Her large, close-set eyes glowed when she smiled.

"Mama, this is Mr. Chandler and Miss Roper from C&R Bank. They say Mr. Carter is dead."

"Oh." She laughed, a high-pitched musical sound. "What wonderful news. But I apologize. Please sit down. I have a sad story, and you must understand why I rejoice in my freedom."

"May I sit here?" Mary Beth motioned to the unoccupied end of the plush sofa.

"Please. I hope you take a pillow. They are ever so comfortable. It's a pleasure to sit with someone who brings such good news."

Mary Beth eased down, amazed at the softness. "Such a lovely room."

"Tell me what happened," Mrs. Harden said.

Peter chose an overstuffed chair right across from Mrs. Harden and gave her the details of Carter's death.

"Oh, then you must hear my story. Confidentially, of course. But first, let me ask for tea." She stood and pulled the bell cord beside the fireplace. "Long discussions flow so much better with a beverage."

A knock on the door interrupted them.

"Another visitor?"

"Yes." Peter leaned forward, placing his hands on his knees. "We expect the sheriff. He is—"

"We are investigating Carter's crimes ..." Mary Beth realized she had interrupted Peter. So much for their good relationship. She would ask forgiveness later.

"Beverly, would you get that, my dear?" Mrs. Harden sat back and closed her eyes. "I must consider where to start my tale. It's a long one. And painful."

"Of course, Mama. And as I go, I shall tell the maid what we need."

"The sheriff will need to hear," Mary Beth said. "I suggest we wait for him."

"Of course." Mrs. Harden smiled. "I shall have more time to remember the details."

The room fell silent, and Mary Beth wished she could think of a suitable topic. The quiet felt awkward. Plus, she had so many questions needing answers.

Beverly returned. "Dr. Smith and the sheriff have come. Please find a seat, gentlemen."

"I prefer to stand," said the sheriff. He came to the end of the couch, crossed his arms and scowled.

"Doctor, I didn't know you planned to come," Mary Beth said.

"I can check on Mrs. Harden and Mr. Weston, who is recovering in the house next door, even though Mrs. Harden seldom needs me these days." The doctor sat in an overstuffed chair by Peter and put his bag beside him.

Miss Harden chose a settee beside the doctor.

Mary Beth turned to the older lady. "Tell us where you met Mr. Carter."

"I shall ask the questions, please." The sheriff cleared his throat. "What do you know about Carter?"

Mrs. Harden turned red and looked down. "He blackmailed me for years."

Mary Beth gasped. "Horrible."

Silence filled the room.

"You must understand how much I detested Mr. Carter." She looked up and sighed. "He … violated me when I was a girl and told me that act made him my husband."

"That brute," the sheriff waved a fist in the air. "If only I could arrest him."

"Mama, you do not have to say more." Beverly rose and walked toward Mrs. Harden.

Mary Beth noticed Mrs. Harden's growing pallor. "I agree with your daughter. We know enough."

"Oh, no." the sheriff crossed his arms again. "I must know what happened today. Did you have anything to do with Mr. Carter's death?"

"Of course not." Mrs. Harden closed her eyes and placed a hand on her throat. "Beverly, please sit down. I'd best tell everything after all these years of pain."

Beverly eased back down on the settee.

"After Carter's unspeakable deed, I was terrified of him and refused to see him, which made him angry." Mrs. Harden swallowed as she picked fringe on the pillow beside her.

"Did you tell your parents?" Dr. Smith asked.

"No." She shrugged. "I feared they would blame me. Years later, I learned that such … violation … isn't the same as marriage, but as a child, I worried someone would find out."

"Naturally." Mary Beth could not imagine such suffering.

"I'm so glad my parents moved the family. All of my fears died down since he didn't threaten me."

"How did you meet up again?" Mary Beth asked as she reached over to squeeze Mrs. Harden's arm. She looked over at the sheriff, and he didn't appear upset she asked another question.

"I later married Mr. Harden who settled here. I was horrified when I learned Mr. Carter lived down the road.

Carter made demands, and I was too afraid to say no because he would tell my secret."

"You should have informed your husband," the sheriff said. "Such men should be prosecuted to the fullest extent of the law."

"Carter threatened to tell my husband if I said anything." She laced her fingers together and sighed. "Carter hinted he would claim I enticed him and call me a lady of the night. I did not want my husband to know. So embarrassing."

Mary Beth longed to slap Carter. How terrible for Mrs. Harden.

"After Carter's father died, his behavior grew more boisterous, and he spent all the money he inherited. He mortgaged the property while claiming he could recover."

"Our records can verify that," Peter said.

"I doubt he tried hard to stop spending, but when money got tight, he asked for money to keep my story quiet. I complied, because I feared for my reputation. He often did mean things to my home, like stealing or damaging something we owned."

"But your husband came to us with information on him. Why?" Peter sat forward in his chair.

"Edward sensed I feared our neighbor, and he finally wormed the horrid details out of me. When he decided to stand up to Carter, things became worse. He claimed he would tell everyone Edward and I never married, and that's when he started breaking into our house and damaging our belongings."

"Why do people keep crime a secret? I'm here to enforce the law, and I could have arrested him." The sheriff's face reddened.

"I lived in fear," Mrs. Harden whispered.

"Carter shouldn't have done any of that." Mary Beth couldn't imagine living with such persecution.

"No." Mrs. Harden shuddered. "Terror choked me anytime my husband probed for the full story. I couldn't bear to lose my reputation even though my husband said he would stand by me."

"The first day I came to visit ..." Mary Beth paused, wondering if she should finish.

"Go on." Mrs. Harden closed her eyes. "I think I know what you are going to ask."

"The odor ..." Mary Beth shivered at the memory and hoped she hadn't made a mistake bringing it up.

Mrs. Harden groaned. "Carter hid a dead animal in a wall of the house. As it decayed, the house smelled ... I hired extra help ... to clean it up."

"Ugh. Mr. Carter deserved his end." The sheriff scowled.

"How do you know Carter did that?" Peter asked.

"He told me." Mrs. Harden said. "He punished me for not giving him cash."

The mention of cash brought Mary Beth's original question. "The day before your husband died, you went to the bank and withdrew money. Later that day, you deposited that same amount."

"Yes." Mrs. Harden coughed. "I had withdrawn money to pay Mr. Carter. My husband said I should stop paying him and told me to put the money back. Carter found out when he came for the cash. He insisted my husband meet him at the bank the next day. When I heard that, I worried, but Edward refused to listen to my warnings."

The sheriff spoke up, "Do you believe Carter killed

your husband?"

"He told me he did." Tears spilled from her huge brown eyes.

"How can you be so sure?" Peter asked. "I didn't see him in the mob at the bank."

"He probably disguised himself." She shrugged. "He mastered trickery."

"How could Carter do that?" the sheriff asked.

"He joined a theater when he was young, and he collected costumes," Mrs. Harden shivered and covered her face with her hands. "It makes me ill to think of it. The makeup he used could alter facial features."

"Could he have been the man stirring up the riot outside our bank?" Mary Beth asked. *What an amazing story.*

"Probably."

"Do you know how Carter killed your husband?" Peter asked.

"Yes. Carter learned to twist the neck just enough to cause it to break. He told me about Edward and threatened to break my neck the same way. I never understood how he killed Edward without anyone seeing what he was doing. My stomach turns when I think about it." Mrs. Harden put her hands over her face. "He moved into my basement after Edward died."

"Did you ever meet Mr. Owen?" Peter asked.

"No. Carter pretended to be Mr. Owen," Mrs. Harden said. "You will find the red wig in the basement."

"What?" Peter's mouth fell open.

"Carter would dress as someone else, adopting different mannerisms and voice. An amazing actor." Mrs. Harden shook her head. "I never saw him onstage, but he was convincing."

"What about the lawyer? Mr. James?" Peter asked. "The alleged Owen claimed he should inherit the property and would sue if we didn't comply with his wishes."

"Carter masqueraded as a lawyer too. At one point, I think he argued a court case," Mrs. Harden said. "Knowing him, he would be pleased to frighten a young banker."

"If Owen actually filed the case, no one would show up in court to prosecute," the doctor said. "You have nothing to fear."

"Owen was heavier," Peter rubbed his neck.

"Padding. Think about it. All three men were about the same height." Mrs. Harden slid forward on the couch and held up her hand. "Height is harder to fake, but he could change that a little with elevated shoes. He could appear shorter if he stooped. But I want to know how he died."

Mary Beth took a moment to share the gory details.

"Enough for tonight." The sheriff stomped to the door. "There's nothing for me to do here."

"How does freedom feel?" Mary Beth asked.

"Except for losing Edward, I am quite happy. How I miss him." Mrs. Harden smiled. "I cannot believe Henry Carter holds no power over me anymore."

"I was aware Mama disliked Carter, but I never heard this story," Miss Harden said. She came toward her mother and hugged her, then perched on the arm of the sofa. "I knew Mama was afraid."

"You were away at school during the worst part, my dear," Mrs. Harden took her daughter's hand in both of hers.

The maid entered the room with a tea tray and muffins.

"I know it's late, but I hope you will join me," Mrs. Harden said. "Miss Roper, would you like sugar?"

"Yes, and a drop of milk." Freedom. Truth. God's word. All things Carter did not value. What a mess he made.

CHAPTER NINETEEN

A pleasant breeze and bright sunshine filtered into the church foyer as Mary Beth stepped outside after the service. The pastor's words resonated in her mind. She intended to go home and talk over the sermon with her father.

"Mary Beth?"

She turned to see Peter coming up beside her. "I keep thinking about how I interrupted you at Mrs. Harden's house last night. I was so anxious to get information. That was rude, and I apologize."

"Actually, I cannot stop thinking about how I did the same thing when you mentioned the bank's name," Peter said as he strolled beside her in the warm weather. "I have been thinking of the bank as mine since I have been running it alone. The fact is, our families share ownership. I hope to catch my tongue before I do that again."

"I assumed you did that because I used the bank's name, so I already forgave you. I probably should have allowed you to introduce us." She smiled up into his face. How pleasant to be able to chat with him like they did years ago.

A big grin covered Peter's face, and the dimple in his cheek appeared. "What did you think about the sermon? Didn't that fit the occasion?"

She nodded. "Yes. What good advice. 'Whatever a man's treasure is, there will his heart be also.' Our hearts should value gold, which is God and his kingdom, or else we make bad choices when the world's values take over."

"Mr. Carter demonstrated what happens when we follow the wrong values," Peter said. "Would you like to share Sunday dinner with us?"

"Oh, Peter." She giggled, allowing her joy to escape. "I would love that, but Papa is still bedridden. Dr. Smith believes the worst is over, and this week, I shall take over his care."

"I understand."

"Maybe you could have dinner with us soon. Papa should be up and about, and I know he wants to talk banking with you." And she wanted to spend time with Peter.

"I accept." His face beamed as he placed a hand on her shoulder.

"Petie!" Peter wanted to gaze forever into Mary Beth's face, but he allowed his hand to fall from her shoulder as his sister came up behind him. "Ruthie, let's race to the curb."

"I'm the youngest, so I get a head start." She took off running and almost fell over her own feet. "Wheee. You can't catch me."

He turned to Mary Beth. "Do you mind if I pause this conversation to tease my little sister?"

"Sure." She laughed. "I shall cheer for you."

How he'd longed for Mary Beth to be part of his team. He dashed past Ruth, touched the curb and ran back. "I won."

"Let's do it again." Ruth said, breathing hard. "I know I shall beat you this time."

"Children." Mrs. Chandler came alongside Mary Beth. "What shall we do with them? Always playing in their Sunday clothes. Why can't they do that during the week?"

"What if we had a tea party in my yard after Sunday dinner?" Mary Beth suggested. "We could wear our older clothes if we wanted to race. I could place Papa in a chair by the window so he could watch."

"What a lovely idea." Mrs. Chandler clapped her hands. "I shall bring cake and cinnamon rolls."

"Yes, like you used to do when we were growing up. Peter, are you okay with that?"

He nodded. "Mother, take my arm. We'll hurry home, so we can party sooner."

VALUING GOLD

About the Author

Cynthia loves younger women and enjoys using new technology to encourage them. She grew up in Chattanooga, TN, where she attended the Erlanger School of Nursing. After she married Ray Simmons, she homeschooled their five children through high school, including her youngest son who has severe disabilities.

Unafraid of tough topics, Cynthia writes The Big Question column for *Leading Hearts* Magazine. In addition, she and her husband host apologetics' discussions with college students over tea.

An avid reader and writer, she served as past president of Christian Authors Guild, teaches writing workshops, and directs the Atlanta Christian Writers Conference.

"Cyndi" adores history and longs to peruse every archive she comes across while traveling. When speaking and teaching, she includes lively vignettes from history and laughs about how she loves women from the past.

She hosts and produces Heart of the Matter Radio and does Cynthia Chats and #momlife encouragement videos. Cynthia loves to help her readers, so visit her Homeschool Answers, which presents one day seminars for homeschool mothers. She also loves to get messages from her readers, so visit her website and leave a message. www.clsimmons. com.

Made in the USA
Columbia, SC
24 October 2020